And then she

Across the room [...] wearing a for[...] sweater, a five [...] half-smile. Ev[...] could *feel* the man's sexual mag[...] wave of rippling heat.

She summoned a jaunty smile that didn't quite make it.

His gaze dipped, checked her out. When his eyes met hers again, she tried to look unfazed, even as another wave of heat sizzled over her...

Dear Reader

A few years ago, fellow Mills & Boon® author Barbara Dunlop and I brainstormed a funny story about two girlfriends who create a Top 10 list of Perfect Boyfriend traits (we're talking in-your-dreams perfect traits, here!). These girlfriends, fuelled by a few late-night margaritas, post their Top 10 list on the Internet and it becomes, to their great surprise, an overnight hit. The list leads to a string of hyped successes (a best-selling paperback, followed by a talk radio show). That novel eventually became THE PERFECT BOYFRIEND by Barbara Dunlop, Book One in this series.

When it came time to brainstorm my sequel, I wondered, What if a guy (my hero, Adam) pens his own rebuttal—a tongue-in-cheek book titled *The Perfect Girlfriend*? And what if he self-publishes his book and it leads to his own competing radio show?

To *really* mix things up, what if Adam ends up in a reality dating show with Cecily? And so was born Book Two in the series, THE PERFECT GIRLFRIEND.

I love to hear from readers—you can write me at Colleen Collins, c/o PO Box 12159, Denver, Colorado 80212, USA. To read about my upcoming releases and to enter monthly giveaways and contests, check out www.colleencollins.net

Happy reading!

Colleen

Recent titles by the same author:

BUILDING A BAD BOY
SWEET TALKIN' GUY

THE PERFECT GIRLFRIEND

BY
COLLEEN COLLINS

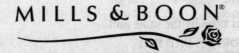

MILLS & BOON®

All the characters in this book have no existence outside the imagination of the author, and have no relation whatsoever to anyone bearing the same name or names. They are not even distantly inspired by any individual known or unknown to the author, and all the incidents are pure invention.

First published in Great Britain 2006
Harlequin Mills & Boon Limited,
Eton House, 18-24 Paradise Road, Richmond, Surrey TW9 1SR

© Colleen Collins 2006

ISBN 0 263 84991 0

Set in Times Roman 10½ on 12¾ pt.
171-0606-45238

Printed and bound in Spain
by Litografia Rosés S.A., Barcelona

THE PERFECT GIRLFRIEND

To Mister Curtiss, AKA Curtiss Bradford, who helped me understand what goes on behind the scenes of a TV show. Any mistakes are the author's, not Mr. C's!

CHAPTER ONE

"GOOD evening, studs…" the male voice on the radio lowered to a husky come-on whisper "…and those babes brave enough to cross over to the dark side."

A soundtrack played a blast of trumpets intermixed with squealing girls' voices.

Cecily Cassell stopped embroidering a small rose on the lapel of a tweed jacket and stared, open-mouthed, at her radio.

"Welcome to *The Perfect Girlfriend*," the male voice continued, "the hippest, hottest, happenest talk-radio show in Denver where you'll learn the score from…" he again dropped his voice to that husky, I-know-what-it's-all-about-baby range "…the man who knows how."

"Just what the world needs," Cecily muttered, tying off a thread. "Another male full of himself."

"I'm your host, Adam MacGruder, owner of *the* best sports bar in town, Home Plate." Another blast of trumpets and squeals. "This is our third show and I know already it's our best because how does a stud approach any situation?"

Cecily reached for a cigarette. "Wearing a sign that says 'I'm an idiot'?"

"With *con-fi-dence*," Adam said, as though he'd personally copyrighted the word. "As I repeatedly tell you in my book, *The Perfect Girlfriend*, con-fi-dence is the rock upon which you build your world. And when you're lucky—'cause studs always get lucky, right?—flashing that con-fi-dence means you'll always be rockin' and rollin' some babe's world, too."

More trumpets and squeals.

Un-frigging-believable. Cecily pushed aside some swatches of fabric, looking for her lighter. *Copied our concept and twisted our title while making a name for himself as the voice for beer-guzzling, babe-ogling men.* Worse, he was a thief. Well, his station was. They'd scheduled Adam's show at the *exact* same time slot as hers, blatantly cutting into her audience.

The show Cecily wasn't at tonight.

No-o-o, she was in her apartment, sewing and smoking because KNOA—desperate to lure listeners back from the dark side—was replaying Cecily and Megan's first interview, the one that had kick-started their own show *The Perfect Boyfriend.* Which was a good thing, really, because Cecily and Megan hadn't just clicked with their audience that night, they'd melded with them. Even Cecily's Grammy Sims, who'd dragged Cecily to church almost every Sunday of her life, called it "a hell of a good time".

Feeling a bit mollified about having the night off, Cecily pushed aside the *Parade* section from last

Sunday's *Denver Post*. Voilà. The plastic orange lighter she'd snagged last week at Bernie's Bagels.

She popped the cigarette into her mouth and flicked the lighter, trying to ignore the background babble of Adam *again* plugging his book.

Normally she wouldn't be caught dead listening to such testosterone-drenched drivel except she'd promised Theodore, KNOA's marketing director and her good pal—or as he called himself her "almost best friend" out of deference to Megan—that she'd listen. Theodore was trying valiantly—and sometimes a tad too dramatically—to pump new life into her radio show. Cecily was willing to work with him, make it happen, but being forced to listen to a solid hour of the Stud Man himself entitled her to a bribe. One pint of extra-spicy guacamole from Hilario's, the best Mexican food restaurant in North Denver. For that, Cecily had promised she'd listen dutifully to Adam's show.

"Don't forget," continued Adam, "you get a five percent discount at the Tattered Cover if you say 'Adam from KHOE sent me' when you buy a copy of *The Perfect Girlfriend*."

She glanced at her watch. *Jeez, on the air mere minutes and he's already plugged his book, what, four times?*

"Studs, time to kick off our show with the best pick-up line of the week. Tonight's was submitted by Danny Copeland of Westminster. And here it is…" Dramatic pause. "Should I call you tomorrow or just nudge you?"

Cecily groaned, wondering if she still had any Tums handy.

"Danny Copeland! Join the Stud Club!" Squeal, no trumpets. "Danny gets a free Guys' Night Out gift package at my bar, Home Plate, corner of Market and Twentieth in the heart of LoDo. Package includes free brewskies, pizza and an autographed copy of my book *The Perfect Girlfriend*, the book that explains the 'three Ms'—how to meet, manage and *not* marry babes."

I could yark. Cecily blew out a gust of cigarette smoke. Although, from what she'd heard, Adam had a string of ladies vying for his attention. *Can't be the personality. Has to be his looks.*

She frowned, trying to recall if she'd ever seen a picture of the man. Nope, except for that giant-sized pencil sketch of his face—which made him look like a jaw with hair on top—that currently graced the sides of city buses. Underneath were the words: Mr Maligned, the voice of the misunderstood male. KHOE. Tuesday nights. 9 p.m.

Mr *Maligned*?

Misunderstood males?

Brewskies, pizzas and the three Ms?

This wasn't talk radio, it was a Neanderthal Meet and Greet.

Should've asked for two *free pints of guacamole.*

Adam was yammering on about his book again, slipping in another, "Say Adam from KHOE sent you and get a five percent discount."

With a roll of her eyes, Cecily turned down the

volume and headed across the room to her CD player, where she slipped in a Sheryl Crow CD. As the words to "My Favorite Mistake" began playing, Cecily checked out her reflection in a hanging mirror. Her birthday was coming up in a month. She'd be twenty-five, a good milestone to invest in colored contacts. Sapphire-blue. Emerald-green. Anything, dear God, to offset her boring brown eyes and brown hair. *Only Cindy Crawford can get by with that brown-on-brown look.*

Cecily took another drag of her cigarette, wishing she hadn't had that Cindy Crawford moment. Such icons of perfectionism were the bane of women's existence. *Next I'll be lifting my shirt and wishing for Gwen Stefani's stomach. Or Madonna's boobs.*

Those impossible rock-star-movie-star role models, and men like Adam, were the *very* reason she and her best pal Megan had, that infamous night a year-plus ago, penned *The Perfect Boyfriend.* It still amazed Cecily how posting their tequila-induced epiphanies on that website, Dating Disasters, had evolved so quickly into a cult following, then a popular handbook, followed by their own Denver talk-radio show, *The Perfect Boyfriend.*

She and Megan had hung on for the ride, enjoying their flash of mini-fame, then—ka-boom—it had ended when Megan had left the show to marry an Irish soccer star.

Although Cecily had grown reasonably skilled on the radio show with her quips and streams of consciousness, what had really kept the show going had been outgoing Megan's non-stop banter.

With only Cecily at the helm, the show's ratings had dropped.

At that point, she would have dropped out, too, and focused on her true goal, Well Suited, the one-woman business she had built re-tailoring "urban-fem" jackets from used men's suits. Unfortunately, thanks to investing most of her book earnings into high-risk gold futures—who would have thought the gold market would unpredictably peak?—she'd effectively wiped out most of her savings. She'd held on to the storefront, right below her apartment here on the Sixteenth Street Mall, as long as she could. But a few months ago, she had had to put up the dreaded "Going Out of Business" sign and terminate her lease.

Which meant *The Perfect Boyfriend* talk show was her sole means of income, and she *needed* to make it work.

Especially after a certain Adam MacGruder had suddenly jumped on the bandwagon with his self-published parody of her and Megan's book. *And* got his own talk show on a competing radio station during *her* time slot. *The Perfect Boyfriend* versus *The Perfect Girlfriend.* Jeez, before this Cecily had thought such he-said-she-said conflicts only happened on cheesy sitcoms or bubble-gum movies starring Meg Ryan and some hunk-actor of the hour.

Guess again.

Beep de beep. Beep de beep.

Cecily checked the caller ID on her cell phone. "Damn," she muttered before punching Talk.

"Hi."

"So whattya think?" asked Theodore.

"I think somebody should tell Adam that con-fi-dence is one word, not three."

Pause. "You're listening to Sheryl Crow."

"I also have the radio on." She flicked her ciga-rette ash over an empty coffee cup. "Sort of."

"You said you'd *dutifully* listen."

"I did. Then I got dutifully nauseous so I turned it down. Do I still get my guacamole?"

Her tabby cat, named "Bob" because of his half tail, hopped onto the table and meowed. Whenever she got on the phone, Bob inevitably thought the con-versation was with him, and proceeded to talk back.

"Look, sweetpea, I know he's a jerk. But he's in, he's hot, and it's *critical* you listen to your compe-tition. We can't let KHOE muscle in any more on our ratings."

"We cater to enlightened women, not men."

Big sigh. "Sweetheart, I hate to burst your bubble, but you and Megan had a *big* male following. Not all were masochists, either. Remember, until recently, our friend Adam hosted a special Guys' Night Out at his bar where he blasted your radio show and pro-vided phones for patrons to call in."

Cecily remembered. Too well. Some of their comments could have frizzed her already curly hair.

"Being forced to listen to 'our friend Adam' is forcing me to smoke again," she muttered.

"Sweetie, you took it up months ago. When Megan left."

"Do all gay men have such good memories?"

"Only for hunks' phone numbers and, for this gay man, any marketing scheme that could boost your show's ratings. Now, you promised to listen to Adam's show. Don't make me beg."

"He sucks," she muttered.

"And don't tease me. Turn down Sheryl and turn up Adam. I'll call you after the show and we'll debrief."

"Wait!"

"What?"

"Do I still get my guacamole?"

"Spicy-hot. *Two* pints. Because I know that's what you'd be pushing for next."

Cecily smiled. "Have I told you lately that you're the perfect man?"

"Yes. And have I told you lately how wise and insightful you are? Now, turn up the volume. And don't cheat. There'll be a pop quiz later. Ciao, sweetpea." Click.

Cecily set down her cell phone, hearing faint scraping and clunking sounds beneath her apartment. A new business was moving into the one-room storefront below.

Well Suited went south. Radio show's headed in the same direction. She looked at Bob, who had plopped himself down on the paper, still staring at her. Times like this, she really missed the days when she and Megan had lived in those great old apartments a few blocks over. No matter how bad a day it had been, there had always been a neighbour willing to tip a margarita or two and commiserate over life's foibles.

"Theodore's right," she said to Bob, who wagged his half tail in response.

"I need to listen to Mr Maligned, understand the competition."

After taking a long, procrastinating drag off her cigarette, she turned up the volume.

"...so let's open the lines and hear from our callers," said Adam. "Tonight, we'll vote on which of the traits from my book, *The Perfect Girlfriend,* best fulfills your perfect girlfriend fantasy. The gal who puts out on date one? Or the gal who, without asking, does the beers-and-brats run to the snack bar at sports events? Lines are open. Call me at 303-555-1556. That's 303-555-1556."

"Advertisers pay good money for this?" she muttered, stubbing out her cigarette.

"Caller number one, you're on the air."

Some guy laughed nervously, sounds of guffawing men in the background. "I'm on?"

"You're on, stud," said Adam. "Go for it."

Stud. Cecily shook her head. *They wish.*

"Gimme a babe who runs for brats any day."

"We got one for the brat babes!" Adam said. "That's 303-555-1556. Keep those votes comin' in. Caller number two, you're on the air."

Cecily debated if she should make a batch of her killer margaritas and numb herself for the rest of this Macho Mouth Fest.

The caller belched. "Puttin' out on date one, man. Get a buddy to do the snack-bar run!"

Heat rushed to Cecily's cheeks. This wasn't entertainment, it was an insult to all women everywhere. She tapped her fingers on the coffee-table, debating whether to light another cigarette.

"We got one for the put-out babes!" Adam enthused, followed by that damn squealing and trumpeting soundtrack.

That did it. Time for someone with a *two*-digit, not one, IQ to call in. She grabbed her cell.

"That's 303-555-1556," said Adam. "Lines are open…"

"Just keep 'em that way," she murmured, punching in the numbers, ready to tangle with testosterone.

Adam MacGruder adjusted the mike as he checked out the computer screen. While a thirty-second advertising spot for Rocky's Autos played, he took a sip of his soda and scanned the list of waiting callers.

Cecily on line five.

He grinned. *A woman caller. First one tonight. Cool.*

He glanced over at the plate-glass window through which he saw Lynn—or "Roz" as he sometimes called her, a play on the character in that TV show *Frasier.* Lynn had on her headphones, screening the calls. When she looked up, he held up his free hand, spreading his fingers wide to indicate the number five.

Lynn nodded, followed by a soulful shake of her short, spiky locks as though already commiserating with poor "Cecily on line five". He'd never understood Lynn's mix of punk hair and Rocky Mountain High wardrobe of faded jeans, Gortex and T-shirts, several decorated with photos of her three kids and hubby who'd recently lost his job. Didn't get her seeming happy with that life, either. A family scrapping by on one salary had to be tough.

That kind of rose-colored point of view reminded Adam of his mother, someone he'd tried in the latter half of his thirty-two years to not second-guess. It was tough to look back, though, and remember her counting spare change to see if they had enough to buy dinner. Smiling as though there were nothing to worry about, claiming his dad would get another contract soon, just you wait and see…

The Rocky's Autos spot was winding down. With a nod, Lynn pointed at Adam, his cue to take the airwaves.

"Welcome back to *The Perfect Girlfriend*," Adam announced, pressing a button.

A blast of trumpets and squeals.

"And speaking of girlfriends," he continued, "our next caller is the first babe brave enough to cross over to the dark side tonight. You're on the air—" Damn, what was her name? He glanced at the monitor. "—Cecily. Go for it."

"Go for it?" she answered. Soft voice, yet he detected an edge.

"Yeah, go for it," coaxed Adam. "As in talk to us. Give us your vote."

"I vote that you treat women with respect."

Whoa, he'd reeled in a Gloria Steinem. He cocked a "watch this" grin at Lynn.

"Trust me, baby, I do," he said, easing his lips so close to the mike he could almost take a nibble. "I treat women with respect as often as they'll let me. R-e-s-p-e-c-t. Like in the ol' Aretha Franklin tune. Give a lady her propers when she gets home, oh, yeah…"

Lynn rolled her eyes, but he caught her smile. They both knew he'd just irked his caller *and* entertained his listeners, which was exactly his goal. Damn, he was good.

"I can't believe how you just twisted what I said."

Let the games begin! "You're right, Cecily." Women loved it when a man agreed with them. "I was playing with you, but the truth is…" He pulled back from the mike and checked the clock. Nine-twenty. He had some time to play even more with Cecily before the next break. "I'm respecting you right now by being open and listening, inviting you to speak your mind." He picked up a pencil and waggled it between his index and middle fingers, the overhead light flashing off his Duke University ring.

Cecily cleared her throat. "First of all, I'd appreciate it if you didn't call me 'babe'."

Tenacious. "Really? But you sound like a babe."

He punched a button. Trumpets and squeals resounded, faded. "But for you," he said quickly, "I'll work hard to change my ways. I'll call you Cecily. Lovely name. Don't hear it often."

A beat of dead air. "I was named after my father's sister."

He noticed she didn't say "aunt". Also noticed her voice was vaguely familiar. Rough-edged, with a touch of honey. "So, Cecily, how do you vote?"

Lynn was holding something up in the window and pointing frantically at its cover. A book? He flashed her a "what?" look. "Should the perfect girlfriend put out on date one," he said into the mike, "or do the snack-bar run?"

"Puh-leaze." Deep exhale. "First of all, a woman doesn't 'put out.' She shares the intimacy—"

"Shares the *what*?"

"And if she chooses to do that on date one," Cecily continued, raising her voice over his interruption, "fine. Preferable if she waits a few dates, though, so she and the man can get to know each other, discover if they share other things such as values, goals. This might be a revelation to you, but sex can be a hell of a lot hotter if the mind is involved, too."

When the lady got going, forget about dead air. Plus, now that she'd taken off a strip, her voice was definitely familiar.

"So you vote for 'Shares intimacy on date one or three, whichever comes first'." He hit the squeal-only button.

Another dead-air moment.

"Just like a male not to listen."

"I'm listening, ba—I mean, Cecily. It's just that I listen with more than my ears. I listen with con-fi-dence." Straight out of his book, chapter three. "Learn from the politicians. Hear enough to steal a few words, then say what *you* want."

"Confidence is one word," she murmured, "not three."

Sassy. He moved his lips closer to the microphone. "Just call me Mr. Maligned, the voice of the misun-derstood male."

"Maligned, my…" Her voice trailed off.

Sassy and worked up. "Excuse me, Cecily? Care to finish your sentence?" Through the glass, he saw Lynn throw up her hands. He grinned, knowing he was instigating strong reactions in his listeners, too. "You disagree that I'm Mr. Maligned?"

"More like Mr. Maladjusted."

"Mr. Maladjusted, hmm?" he whispered in his best give-it-to-me-baby voice. "See, here I am ac-tively listening again. In fact, you're sounding more and more familiar to me. Ever drop by my bar, Home Plate?"

"No."

"Not even for Wednesday nights' wet T-shirt con-tests?"

"Dream on."

"Attend one of my book signings for *The Perfect Girlfriend*?"

"About as many as you attended for my book, *The Perfect Boyfriend*."

The Perfect—? He looked over at Lynn, who was waving that book again with an "I told you so" look on her face.

Bingo!

No wonder Cecily's voice was so damn familiar.

"Cecily Cassell," he crooned, "how *perfect* is it that you called!" The phone lines were blinking like flash lightning. "Studs and babes, our caller is none other than the co-author and former co-host, now so-lo-host, of *The Perfect Boyfriend*, the book and show that inspired me to write *The Perfect Girlfriend.* As many of my fans will recall, I used to host a Guys' Night Out every Tuesday at this very time slot where studs got drinks half off while they listened to that retro-feminist show—"

"Hardly retro," interrupted Cecily.

"You're right. Male-bashing never really went out of vogue, did it?" He hit the trumpets button to cover Cecily's expletive. "Sorry, Cecily, I was a little rough there. Seriously, you wrote a tongue-in-cheek guide to dating men, and I followed up with an in-your-face rebuttal."

"*Touché.*"

He smiled to himself. So they agreed on *something*.

"So, Cecily, what's happenin'? Calling while on break from your own show?"

"Tonight's a re-broadcast." She didn't offer more.

He'd heard they were having problems holding on

to their listeners, thanks in part to the growing success of his show. He glanced at the switchboard's flashing lights. Listeners were digging this….

She'd probably be surprised to know that he felt for her situation. He never liked to see anyone struggle. On the other hand, he didn't run a sports bar without understanding people loved watching competitions, especially hard-played ones. Bottom line, that was what it was all about, whether on the playing field, the dating scene or on a radio show.

"Cecily, babe, back to your calling me mal-mal-a—"

"Maladjusted. And I asked you not to call me ba—"

"*Maladjusted!* That's right! Now, why would you call a sweet, laid-back and pretty darn cute guy like me something like that?"

"Because you're asking your listeners to vote on women putting out—"

"Glad you brought up the vote thing again, Cecily! Because, hey, *I* vote you prove your argument. *Prove* I'm maladjusted rather than misunderstood. Listeners, you agree? Shouldn't Cecily Cassell, author and host of *The Perfect Boyfriend*, back up her claim and prove I'm maladjusted?"

"This is ridic—"

"Cecily, Cecily," he whispered huskily into the microphone as though nobody else existed in the world but the two of them. "Isn't your book about empowering women?" He glanced at Lynn who was frantically pointing at the clock. They needed to run an advertising spot, pronto.

"Yes, but—"

"Doesn't your book steal a line from W. C. Fields and say 'Never give a sucker an even break'?"

"Yes, but—"

Lynn was darn near banging her head on the window.

He dropped the sultry it's-just-you-and-me-babe voice. "Then why're you giving me an even break, Cecily? Prove your cause! Empower yourself and all women! Prove I'm maladjusted!"

"Yes, b—"

"Yes! I listened and I heard your answer! I asked you in the beginning to 'go for it', and you just did, babe! Thank you, Cecily, have a great night, talk to you soon, hmm?" He hung up her line.

"Studs and babes," he continued, making a "hold on just one more moment" gesture at Lynn, "Cecily Cassell has taken the gauntlet to prove her claim. Can Ms Perfect Boyfriend prove Mr Perfect Girlfriend is also Mr Maladjusted? Tune in next week and find out the score from…" he pointed at Lynn, telling her to start the commercial "…the man who knows how."

The music for a local bank commercial began playing.

Adam stripped off his headset, grabbed his soda and took a long swig, loving the sweet taste of victory. Because he'd win, no doubt about it. Just had to figure out the rules of this particular game, first.

He set down his soda and grabbed the pencil. Jotted down "call Jerry," his roommate in college who was now a successful TV director in LA. No doubt Jerry could connect Adam with someone, set up some "maladjusted" publicity gig. It'd help his show, boost book sales. If Cecily played it right, exercised some con-fi-dence, she'd get a piece of the action, too.

He was jotting down some more notes when Lynn motioned he'd be back on the air soon.

He nodded, slipped on his headset and took a last sip of soda. *Maladjusted.* He chuckled to himself. *Cecily Cassell, you didn't insult me, you inspired me.*

This game was going to be fun....

CHAPTER TWO

AN IRRITATING sound, like a bicycle bell gone amok, penetrated Cecily's sleep. Groggily, she squinted open one eye and stared blearily at the pile of magazines and assorted drinking glasses that covered her nightstand.

Brrring. Brring.

Somewhere in that pile was her phone.

Pawing aside a magazine and part of a glazed donut, she glanced at the alarm clock. Seven-thirty. Who in their right mind called at this ungodly hour? Better be a family or girlfriend emergency.

Brrring. Brring.

She fumbled for the receiver. "Hullo?"

"Good morning!"

An unfamiliar man's voice.

"Yes?" she croaked.

"This is *your* lucky day!"

Real lucky, all right. She'd started her day with an adrenalin-crazed telemarketer at the crack of dawn.

"Goodbye."

"Cecily, wait! This isn't a sales call!"

He knows my name. "Who's this?" Bob, thinking she was talking to him, jumped onto the covers and meowed in her face.

"My name's Kevin Donovan. I'm the assistant producer on the television show *Marriage Material...or Misfortune?* Have you seen it?"

She scratched Bob behind his ear, and his purr engine chugged to life. She was a *CSI* junkie, and occasionally watched CNN, but that was it on the TV front. However, callers into her radio show had mentioned *Marriage Material...or Misfortune?*, which she understood was a reality show where cameras followed two conflicted individuals in a series of dates from hell.

She thought those reality shows where people were stranded on a desert island and ate bugs to stay alive sounded far more sane.

"You want me to interview one of the show's couples on *The Perfect Boyfriend* radio show?"

"Oh, no. We want *you*, Cecily."

It took a moment for the words to sink in. "What?"

"Yes, we want you and Mr Adam MacGruder to star in five episodes, each a mystery date in Denver at a location to be picked by the show. And what's perfect about it—"

"What?" She bolted upright. Bob scurried to the far end of the bed.

"That's right," Kevin enthused, "The Stud Man and the Feminist. The opinionated authors of *The*

Perfect Girlfriend and *The Perfect Boyfriend*, dating each other. The audience will eat it up."

"I'd rather eat bugs," she murmured, fumbling for the crumpled pack of cigarettes on her nightstand.

"What?"

"Wait a minute, I get it." She smiled. "I'm being punk'd, right?" By none other than Theodore. He was up too early as usual at his favorite Starbucks, wired on a triple-shot mocha-caramel-something latte, thinking what a hoot it'd be to wake up ol' Sweetpea Cecily like this. Probably paid some guy ten bucks to make the call. Ha ha. Real funny.

"No," Kevin said, "I'm not punking you."

"Yeah, right, and I'm Demi Moore. Put Theodore on the phone." She scanned the area for her lighter.

"No, I'm *really* Kevin Donovan from *Marriage Material...or Misfortune?* Perhaps you'll believe me if you check your caller ID? Two-one-three is the area code for Los Angeles."

She brushed aside a Patricia Cornwell paperback and squinted at the digital display. A small chill shot through her as she read the number. Two-one-three, five-five-something...Los Angeles, all right. The city she'd moved from two years ago with a puce-colored couch, one thoroughly pissed-off cat and a headful of dreams about love and happy-ever-after.

She still had the couch and the cat.

"Cecily?"

"Present." Unfortunately.

"What's *perfect* for each of you is that during the

dates you'll be pitting your *Perfect Boyfriend* and *Perfect Girlfriend* book rules against each other."

She snapped the lighter and lit her cigarette.

About the *last* thing that sounded perfect on this planet was force-dating a macho-megalomaniac who owned a *sports bar* that had weekly *wet T-shirt contests*, for God's sake. This was hardly what she and Megan had envisioned when they'd penned their rules for *The Perfect Boyfriend.* They'd wanted to encourage women to stand up for their rights, their integrity!

"What do you think?" asked Kevin.

I think your proposition is like asking Gloria Steinem to date shock-jock Howard Stern.

Not that Cecily didn't have a streak of impulsiveness—like the time in high school when she cut her hair in a Mohawk on a dare—but dating a Neanderthal on live television? She'd rather go on a dozen bad dates in real life than humiliate herself even *once* publicly like that.

Wait a minute, didn't people win prizes—like money—on that show?

She blew out a stream of blue smoke. "I'm listening."

"Our last show got a fifteen percent share, which equates to approximately ten million viewers. That's a lot of free publicity for your book. *Now* what do you think?"

"Give me a moment…"

Okay, numbers she could handle. *Ten million.* If only two percent of the audience bought her book, it had a good chance of hitting a bestseller list, which had always been her and Megan's dream. Their sales for *The Perfect Boyfriend* had been impressive, but unfortunately they'd never—in the words of their former publicist—"hit the lists".

She took another puff, wondering if publicly humiliating oneself justified increased book sales. Which pissed her off to even ponder it. Nobody would ever place her idol, Patricia Cornwell, in such a quandary.

"Besides the book publicity factor," Kevin continued, "there's the *twelve thousand dollars. Now* how does that sound?"

But then, she wasn't exactly Patricia Cornwell. Public humiliation, potential mega book sales *and* twelve grand chump change? She flicked the cigarette in an ashtray while Bob flopped over onto his back and twisted his head at what had to be a painful angle to stare at her.

"It *sounds* good," Cecily muttered, emphasizing the word "sounds", a word apart from "is".

"After each show," Kevin explained, "the audience votes for who best outwitted, manipulated or slam-dunked the other in the dating game."

Slam-dunked. What was it with men and sports metaphors? They got to first, second and third base with a girl. They slam-dunked a situation.

"But even though it's a competition, it's a win-win for both you and Adam. You'll be paid for the time worked on the show plus free book publicity. Do I hear a yes?"

No. "The publicity has potential," she conceded, "but you and I both know the only guarantee is twelve grand salary—"

"Oh, no," Kevin interrupted. "Twelve grand is what the *winner* takes home. All that's guaranteed is the Screen Actors Guild base salary for appearing in each episode, as well as the free book publicity."

Base salary translated to "not much". The rest of the words washed over her except for one. *"Winner?"*

"Correct. Whoever gets the most votes at the end of five episodes is the winner."

"The viewers' votes are for whoever—" *is the best actor and snows the viewers* "—is the most persuasive."

"Correct."

"I'm not an actor."

"Neither is Mr MacGruder."

Oh, yes, he is. If anybody was a born ham, it was that male. Unfortunately, Cecily was about as un-ham as they came. That was why she had been such a good team with Megan. On the radio show, Cecily had been able to sit back, let Megan charm and entertain listeners, and all Cecily had had to do was chime in with a glib comment or two when the mood struck.

But *act*? The most acting she'd ever done was as one of the three wise men in her second grade Christmas play, and that was only because Robbie Emerson got the flu.

"I don't think this will work," she muttered.

"Sure it will. This is a reality show. Nobody expects you to act or pretend to be anyone but yourself, Cecily.

Hey, how many times in life does someone come along and offer you fame and fortune and all you have to be is yourself?"

"Well, it almost happened with *The Perfect Boyfriend*—"

"That's why reality shows are so popular—people want to see people like themselves in real-life situations."

"People don't want to see me."

"Sure they do. You're, as your book title says, *perfect.*"

"Spare me."

"It's true. Only the author of *The Perfect Boyfriend* can go up against the author of *The Perfect Girlfriend.*"

"Megan would've been perfect, not me. If we were Penn and Teller, I'd be Teller."

"Huh?"

"You know, those magicians. One of them never talks—I think that's Teller. Anyway, not that I never talk, but I'm definitely not the flash you want."

"Who's talking flash? You're sincere. Which equates to *real.* As in *reality* TV."

If he wanted to talk real, dates from hell were definitely that. Maybe if she'd had a chance to win twelve grand for going on one of many in her past, her current financial situation wouldn't be so bad.

Not that she was caving in, but it wouldn't hurt to check the numbers. She grabbed a pen off her nightstand and jotted down a few numbers on the back of a magazine. *Let's see...* Winner's take would buy approximately five-six months of inventory, work time, publicity, distribution, miscellaneous odds and ends.

That was, *if* she were the winner. If she weren't, she'd make some kind of base salary, which sounded ominously like peanuts, plus risk ending up the laughing stock of millions of faceless people in TV-land.

"Sorry, but the answer's no."

"Don't forget those potential books sales—"

"Kevin, at this point in my life, I want to know what's guaranteed, not what's possible."

"All right." His voice dropped to a more serious range. "What if the prize were fifteen grand?"

"Uh, no."

"Twenty?"

Nearly *double* the original prize? That meant almost a year she could invest her time and energy into rebuilding Well Suited. Maybe being followed by cameras on a few weird dates wasn't all that bad....

"Twenty-five?"

"Well, yes, it sounds good—"

"Great! Our legal department will draw up the contract and get back to you."

"Wait, I said *sounds* goo—"

A dial tone buzzed in her ear.

An hour and two diet colas later, Cecily Cassell hated her life.

She'd spent ten minutes on the phone with her Grammy Sims, a diehard fan of reality shows who couldn't stop gushing about her granddaughter being a star on one. Cecily loved her Grams, had grown especially close to her while living at her Silverlake home while attending UCLA, but just for once wished her grandmother wouldn't be her staunchest supporter.

Cecily next called Theodore. Surely Theodore, who'd dated his fair share of jerks, would understand her revulsion to publicly date a Macho Mental Midget. However, on the where-can-I-get-empathy scale of one to ten, with ten mega-empathy, Theodore was a one. He'd barely heard she'd been invited to be on *Marriage Material...or Misfortune?* before he started shrieking that it was a fabulous, absolutely fabulous, idea that would sky-rocket *The Perfect Boyfriend* radio-show ratings.

Feeling bleak, she called the last person she truly trusted. A friend who was a constant voice of reason in a chaotic world. Megan.

Megan heard her out, empathized how most men—except when you find The One—were cads, commiserated over the state of dating in a survivor-mentality world...

...then claimed she absolutely *loved* the idea of Cece being on *Marriage Material...or Misfortune?*

Too stunned to respond, Cecily listened as Megan said Cece would be a fool to pass up such a fantastic PR opportunity. So what if she was dating the biggest Neanderthal in Denver? It was a primo opportunity to promote their Perfect Boyfriend philosophies and stand up for women's rights! Not to mention their book would undoubtedly end up on *The New York Times* bestseller list, their dream come true!

After hanging up, Cecily decided it was not in her best interest to call anyone else. Instead, she had a heart to heart with Bob who, with a belly full of kibbles, preferred to lounge lazily in the kitchen window rather than listen.

"Just like a man to put himself first," she muttered as she rummaged through swatches of material and cereal boxes for her cell phone. "Maybe Megan pulled off the public-dating thing—jeez, even marrying the guy—but that's not my style. I'm the introverted type. The kind of woman who likes being *behind* the scenes and not in front of the cameras." She groaned, thinking if cameras added ten pounds, she'd need to lose *twenty* to look normal.

No, no more calling for emotional support. She needed to go to the source.

A minute later, she was punching in the number to the LA production offices of *Marriage Material...or Misfortune?*

"Kevin Donovan. May I help you?"

"Cecily Cassell. Look, Kevin, I really appreciate the offer, but—"

"Cecily, hon, glad you called. Listen, I'm on the other line. Let me transfer you to our production assistant, Roger, who's handling all the details and can answer your questions."

A few moments later, a peppy male voice came on the line. "Roger here. How can I help you?"

"Kevin transferred me to you. My name's Cecily Cassell and, although I appreciate the offer, I'm actually an introverted person—"

"Cecily, great to meet you! All the ducks are in a row."

Ducks?

"Adam's show is already working on the ad campaign 'Clash of the Perfects'. And your radio show in Denver, which I understand has been sweating falling ratings, has jumped on the bandwagon with their own campaign 'Beauty Battles the Beast'."

While she'd been calling her nearest and dearest in a vain attempt for empathy and support, Kevin and his team had been heating up the phone lines, too, making this a done deal.

"As you're probably aware, besides viewers voting after each segment with the grand tally deciding who's the winner, after the last show there'll be a separate, one-time vote on whether the two of you are marriage material!"

Just when she'd thought life couldn't suck enough.

"Cecily, babe, gotta run. Listen, you'll be perfect, just like your book, *The Perfect Girlfriend*!"

Babe? "Perfect *Boyfriend*—"

"Trust me!"

Click.

As if she hadn't heard that line before.

With a sinking feeling in her stomach, she realized she was in a corner. Her radio station was all pumped up, building a damn ad campaign. Beauty Battles the Beast.

"I'm screwed," she muttered, dragging her feet toward the kitchen. Maybe there was something in the refrigerator that could offer comfort in this dark hour.

She stood in front of her open refrigerator, surveying her comfort resources: a carton of eggs, package of something green she didn't want to ponder too long, enough bottles of condiments to stock a hot-dog stand, a token piece of fruit and a package of Twinkies.

As she reached for the latter it suddenly dawned on her that, just as two Twinkies were packaged together, two people were packaged into this dating arrangement. If said two people were a solid front, what could the show do?

Suddenly she knew how to stop this love locomotive before it even left the station.

Nine hours later, at five-thirty p.m. sharp, the regulars started arriving for their nightly happy hour at Home Plate. Wednesdays were a high spot because in three hours the weekly Wednesday wet T-shirt contest began.

"Adam, my man, how's your new Eve?" said Rodney, settling his round frame onto a corner stool next to Larry, the youngest of the regulars who'd arrived a few minutes earlier. From the far room came the sharp click of balls in a pool game.

"Getting ready, no doubt, to tempt me." Adam poured beer from a tap.

"With an apple?"

"You're talking to the Stud Man." Adam slid the glass of beer across the bar top to Rodney. "Think I fall for that old wanna-bite-of-apple line?"

Tom, a dour-faced attorney who'd started dropping by a year ago after his divorce, walked heavy-footed to a seat. "Not even for the right woman?" he asked in his baritone voice.

"What's *right*," Adam answered, tossing a high-ball glass from one hand to the other, "versus what's *perfect*? The perfect Eve would tempt me with an apple pie, homemade, piping hot."

Rodney chortled, lifted his glass. "You're our inspiration, Adam."

"So, what's this I hear about a TV show?" asked Tom, neatly folding his camel-hair jacket across the stool next to him.

"*Marriage Material...or Misfortune?* wants me and *The Perfect Boyfriend* author to star in a series of dates. Filming starts in a month." He dropped a twist of lemon into the drink and set it in front of Tom.

Rodney checked out a couple of giggling twenty-somethings racking up a game. "You goin' Hollywood on us, Adam?"

"Call me Brad Pitt, boys." He leaned against the back of the bar and crossed his arms over his Allman Brothers 2003 Tour T-shirt. "Y'know, I may run the best sports bar in town. Date the hottest ladies. But one thing's missing from my life..."

The men grew silent, listening.

"Our own baseball team, boys!"

Clapping and laughter.

"Yessiree, with the money I win from *Marriage Material...or Misfortune?*—because I will decimate the competition, no question—I'm going to fund our gear, suits and, best of all, free beers and brats for everyone after each game until the money runs out."

"Our man knows his priorities!"

"Here, here, Adam Stud Man!"

He grabbed a bar towel and dried a glass. "Our jerseys will say Home Plate on the front, MacGruder's Marauders on the back. Our slogan will be one of my rules from *The Perfect Girlfriend*. Free beer to whoever can guess which one."

"The perfect girlfriend does snack-bar runs?" asked Rodney.

"Not quite," said Larry, looking up from his PalmPilot. "It'd be man's top three priorities."

"Free brewski to our grad student!" Adam said, giving a thumbs-up to Larry. "It'll list the three Bs. Brats, beer and babes."

Whoops. Whistles.

"Hey, Mr Hollywood!" called out a suited guy as he stepped inside the front door, holding it open for a woman.

The guys called out greetings.

"Vince, dude!" called out Rodney.

"Get that promotion?" asked Tom, swirling his drink.

"Next time you see me, call me vice president," said Vince, slapping Tom on the back as he headed for an empty stool. As he straddled the seat he called out to Adam, "You gonna become a big movie star and forget your buddies, the little people?"

"Of course," Adam said in mock seriousness, "but I'll still send Christmas cards."

His and Vince's friendship went back to Duke University where they'd been best pals. After wrapping up his finance degree, Adam had moved to Denver for a telecom mid-management job. Within a few months, he'd convinced Vince to interview for another position at the company. Adam had eventually got the entrepreneurial bug and left to start Home Plate. Vince had stayed, working his way up the corporate ladder.

"Good show last night," Vince said, loosening his tie. "Poor Cecily has probably spent the day regretting ever picking up the phone and dialing you."

Rodney wiped the back of his hand across his mouth. "What she look like?"

"Probably like a librarian with an ax to grind," said Adam, tossing the towel over his shoulder. "You know the look. Long skirts, no shape and that tense, 'where's the Maalox?' look on her face."

"Don't break her heart, Adam!" chortled Rodney.

"She'll never be the same after a taste of our Stud Man," said Vince with a laugh.

Adam leaned back against the bar and grinned. "Which is why I'm changing my on-air handle to Mr Misfortune, which I'm stealing from the TV show, because I'm gonna be one misfortunate dude having to date that dominatrix librarian and her book of uptight rules."

"Probably hasn't been on a date in years," added Tom.

"Like you," joked Rodney.

Larry punched something into his PalmPilot. "I calculate Adam has a seventy-five-percent chance of winning."

"Hey," Vince said, nodding his thanks as Adam slid him a beer. "Who wants to place money on our man winning this TV-show competition?"

Rodney pulled out his wallet. "Twenty on Adam."

"I'll double that," said Tom. "Betting's illegal in this jurisdiction, my friends, so let's call it buying insurance on a sure outcome."

As Rodney collected money Adam looked over at the woman who'd followed Vince inside.

She wore a funky tweed and lace jacket, but the rest of the package—denim skirt, black leggings, patent leather heeled boots—gave her a schoolgirl-Emma-Peel look.

Her large dark eyes stared down the room as though it might bite her. He'd seen that look before, knew what it meant.

"Honey," he called out, "you're early. Wet T-shirt contest doesn't start until eight-thirty."

The woman made a snort of derision that turned the guys' heads.

"I'm not here for that," she said. "I'm looking for Adam MacGruder."

Adam slid a look to the guys. "Aren't they all?" he said under his breath.

Laughter.

"Well, it's your lucky day, babe, because you found him. I'm Adam MacGruder, at your service." He bowed.

Was it his imagination, or had she flinched when he'd said "lucky day"?

After boring a small hole through his skull with her stare, she headed to the bar. Holding out her hand, she said, "I'm Cecily Cassell."

Adam had never seen so many guys get suddenly preoccupied with their drinks.

He was a bit taken aback at her firm handshake. And those flashing dark eyes that telegraphed she'd heard way more than he'd ever intended for Cecily Cassell to hear before their first date.

He scraped his knuckle across his chin. "Sorry for, uh, everything you heard."

She gave him a look he couldn't decipher.

"You did, uh, hear everything, right?" Maybe he didn't need to apologize.

"Let's just say it doesn't surprise me."

One of the guys muttered, "Loser moment." Another choked trying to stifle a laugh.

Cecily notched up her chin. "Can we talk?"

"Sure."

"In private."

"What could possibly be private after that?"

She gave him a look.

"I mean, sure, let's talk in private."

He'd invite her to his office in the back, but plunking her down in a room whose walls were decorated with posters of Pamela Anderson Lee and Nicole Smith wouldn't exactly set the right ambience.

"I'm working the bar for the next few hours, so I should stay within sight of it…" Avoiding the guys' looks, he gestured to an empty window seat across the room. "Let's step over there…"

A few minutes later, they sat on either side of a small round table. The window offered a view of Sixteenth Street Mall, the lights going on in shops as daylight waned. People, bundled up against the October cold, walked briskly down the street. In the window hung a Red Hare beer sign, a dapper rabbit perched on a beer keg, outlined in red neon.

"Adam," Cecily said, her voice dropping, "I'll cut to the chase. That TV show will make us look like fools. Let's do something else to publicize our books rather than lose face in front of millions of people."

He thought for sure her first words would be about him and the boys making fun of her, not "cutting to the chase" about *Marriage Material…or Misfortune?* He thought how last night she had zeroed in with what was on her mind, just as she was doing now. He was accustomed to guessing, and double-guessing, what was going on in women's heads, not being told point-blank.

"But viewers will love the show because they love our books."

The neon sign heated the air with crimson, the color playing evocatively with her features. Set her dark curls on fire, added sensuality to her pert nose and full lips. He imagined how that light would play on the rest of her body…

She leaned forward and he caught a whiff of floral scent. "Our books were meant to be read, not acted out *by us.*"

"Even Clint Eastwood acts in his own movies."

"Oh, please," she muttered, "this isn't Make My Day."

She'd shifted in such a way that her jacket fell open, exposing a stretchy T-shirt that revealed small, pert breasts. He'd always been a breast man, the bigger the better, but hers suddenly seemed just the right size.

"I beg to differ," he said, propping his elbows on the table, closing the space between them. "Viewers will love connecting our faces to our book titles. Why do you think people flock to book readings?"

"A famous author reading is a hell of a lot different than you and I cavorting on bogus dates, using our rules like battle weapons." Her nostrils flared slightly, which he was sure she did to show her disapproval, maybe even distance him, but it only spiked his interest.

Still, business was business.

"Since you like cutting to the chase, let's do just that." He leaned back, crossing his arms across his chest. "I signed my contract this afternoon. My radio station has already started a major marketing campaign to advertise my starring on the TV show. Advertising is big bucks, plus people's jobs on the line. You back out, and KHOE will sue you *and* your station."

She gasped, straightened. "On what grounds?"

"Any and all and some we'll make up just to piss you off. Bottom line, Cecily, we'll both benefit from the publicity, but only you will get hurt by a major lawsuit." He cocked an eyebrow. "And from what I've heard, you don't exactly have the means to take on a legal battle."

She gave him a look. "So you've heard about my bad investment."

"Get sweet-talked by a stockbroker?"

She started to nod, stopped herself.

"So I'm right." He winked. "As usual."

With a huff of indignation, she shoved back her chair and stood. After flashing him a go-to-hell look, she marched for the door.

When she reached it, she hesitated, then turned.

"Adam MacGruder," she said with a roll of her shoulders, "get ready to kiss that twenty-five grand goodbye because I'm going to beat your ass."

CHAPTER THREE

ONE month later, fortified with false bravado and a pack of cigarettes tucked into her designer knock-off bag, Cecily walked into trendy Appetites, the kind of place she'd normally never be caught dead in, for her first date. Oh, it was upscale and swanky with its sleek chrome and wood interior, state-of-the-art appetizers and drinks, and take-me-home waiters.

But, bottom line, it was a meat market.

Why women thought such places were a breeding ground for true love left Cecily dumbfounded. In her not-so-humble opinion, which she'd shared on the radio show, going to a bar to meet a nice guy was like going to a morticians' convention to meet a comedian.

The place was abuzz with conversations, colored lights, the clanking and scraping of equipment being moved. From the placement of the cameras, it appeared the highly polished oak bar in the middle of the room would be center stage.

Center stage.

Millions of viewers.

She ran a sweaty palm down the side of her denim hip-hugger skirt, praying the chicken and green chili burrito she'd eaten for lunch stayed down.

A cluster of twenty-somethings, all wearing spandex with booby-flashing necklines, posed around the bar. Cecily frowned. What—did they ship in extras from Hollywood? In her knee-length denim skirt, pink "Get the Party Started" T-shirt, and one of her favorite Well Suited jackets, she looked like a nun in comparison. A *trendy* nun, but still.

When the going got tough, the tough copped a cig.

As she shakily lighted a cigarette a kid with cropped hair and a dazzling white grin made a beeline for her.

"Cecily?"

She blew out a puff. "Yes?"

"Roger."

Roger…Roger…

"The show's production assistant. We spoke on the phone a month ago."

"Right. The production assistant." *Who doomed me to this lower rung of hell.*

She extended her free hand. They shook.

"Welcome. Is there anything I can get you? Water? Soda?"

A new life on a different planet. "No, thanks."

Roger held out a bound notebook. "Here's your script."

She stared it down. "Script?"

"The director wants you and Adam to have a road

map to fall back on, just in case. We meant to get it to you sooner, but the writers didn't finish until late yesterday." He laughed under his breath. "You know how writers are."

"Not really." The only writers she knew were she and Megan and, after their big sale, they were borderline obsessive-compulsive to get everything in on time, if not early.

She accepted the script. "I told Kevin I'm not an actor."

"Hey, not to worry," Roger said, patting her arm. "Like I said, it's just a road map. The words will also be on the teleprompter, so no need to memorize."

What the hell was a teleprompter?

She tapped her finger on the cover, flicking cigarette ash on it. "I—I thought this dating thing was about pitting the rules of our books against each other."

"Sure."

"Did the people who wrote this script read our books, know our rules?"

"I assume so."

"Because that would color their words, wouldn't it? I mean, this whole *thing*—" she dipped her head to indicate the room, the people, the cameras "—is about pitting the caveman against an emancipated woman, correct? Brawn versus brains sort of thing."

Cecily heard the building hysteria in her voice but couldn't have stopped it if she tried. "Speaking of brawn or brains, are the writers men or women? Because, unless there's been some proactive consciousness-raising, chances are high that stereotypical cultural behaviors will creep into a writer's philosophy, don't you agree? And in all fairness, I'm talking about men *and* women, although, yes, probably more men, but that's just the way it is and I wish to hell I hadn't eaten that burrito for lunch because my stomach is starting to do the rumba—"

"I'll, uh, get the director," murmured Roger, backing away with a horrified look and blending into the crowd.

She bent over and squashed her cigarette into the dirt of a potted palm. Maybe not the classiest move, but she was too freaked out to ask for an ashtray. Besides, the room was growing increasingly stuffy and claustrophobic, and no doubt her naturally curly hair was frizzing thanks to the flop sweat drenching her skull.

A trendy nun having a massive meltdown. Gee, how cool could she get?

And then she saw him.

Across the room, Adam leaned against the bar, wearing a form-fitting black turtleneck sweater, a five o'clock shadow and a wicked half-smile. Even from across the room, she could *feel* the man's sexual magnetism. Like a wave of rippling heat.

She summoned a jaunty smile that didn't quite make it.

The room suddenly felt even more crowded, but not from all the people milling about. It was *them*. As though the world receded because their personalities and energy took up more than their share of space.

His gaze dipped, checked her out. When his eyes met hers again, she tried to look unfazed even as another wave of heat sizzled over her.

Crazy. This was crazy. Hadn't she just made some kind of stream-of-consciousness women's dating equality speech to what's-his-face?

She sucked in a fortifying breath. *I'm in control. Twenty-five thousand big ones are at stake and no way that president of the Stud Club male is going to trick me into thinking he likes me, finds me attractive.*

Oh, yeah, she got his scam. This was what she and Megan had pegged "the ol' sex god act". Mr Too Good to Be True—too handsome, too rich, too whatever—the kind of heart-stopping male every woman secretly fantasized about locked gazes with you across a crowded room, making you think you were The One.

Ha!

She rolled back her shoulders, pleased she had nailed that con at the outset. Plus, if she remembered correctly, didn't he discuss this technique in his rip-off, *The Perfect Girlfriend*? If she wasn't mistaken, it was number twenty-three in some pick-up checklist.

When trolling for the perfect girlfriend, which in this book means the perfect one-night stand, dress the part. Studs, write this down: *Women are suckers for black turtlenecks*. Add to that an across-the-room I-want-you-bad stare, and, trust me, within a matter of hours you'll be asking her what she wants for breakfast.

Trolling.

A voice distracted her.

"Darling!" called out a fifty-something slender gentleman, wearing baggy pants and a black silk shirt that coordinated with his pencil-thin mustache and dyed-to-match hair.

"Welcome!" he said, air-kissing her. "I'm Bradley Crown, your director."

The director. Wonderful. Now she could resolve the script issue.

"Mr Crown," she said, summoning her best professional air, "about this—"

"Felicity's look is all wrong," he murmured to an Avril Lavigne look-alike who had materialized next to his side. "Can you *please* do *something* with her?"

"Uh, my name's Cecily."

"Didn't *anyone* tell her how to dress?" he continued to Avril.

"I called and gave her clear instructions," she answered.

This had to be the girl—Tiffany somebody—from Wardrobe who'd called Cecily a week ago and asked her to please wear blue and orange because they showed up well on television. Cecily had informed her those were the Denver Broncos' team colors and she'd wear one or the other, but not both together because the last thing she wanted to do was look like a football groupie.

Cecily gestured to her denim skirt. "I'm wearing blue—"

"Your instructions weren't all *that* clear, it appears," Bradley murmured, looking Cecily up and down. "Tiffany, darling, please get Delores over here to fix her. We go live in two hours."

As Tiffany minced away on elevator heels Bradley glanced down to Cecily's hands.

"I see you got your script."

"Mr Crown," she said, steeling herself, "I was never told I'd be memorizing anything. *Especially* right before I go on the air. Besides, this show's conflict is based on what's in our books, the rules of *The Perfect Boyfriend* versus *The Perfect Girlfriend*—"

When he waved his fingers dismissively, a diamond-studded Rolex sparkled on his wrist. Jeez, maybe she should become a Hollywood director.

"The script is merely a guideline, darling, nothing to worry about. Same words are on the teleprompter."

"What's a teleprompter?"

He gestured toward what looked like a portable TV monitor nearby. "The words scroll slowly down, easy to read. It'll always be within viewing distance. Just look for the red light on top of the screen."

"I can't be real and read at the same time!"

"Darling, we don't want you to *read*. Just nonchalantly glance at the teleprompter occasionally to be sure you're on track. It's merely a safety net."

He eyed the squashed cigarette in the dirt of the potted palm. "One last note. No smoking on camera. We don't want a haze covering your pretty face."

An older woman, her graying hair pulled back in a ponytail and a cigarette dangling from her over-red lips, approached them. Around the neck of her sweatshirt dangled a tape measure.

"Problem, Brad?" she asked in a smoke-cured voice, looking slightly bored and pissed off at the same time.

"Delores, she looks like Pippy Longstockings Does San Quentin."

As Cecily gasped, too stunned to respond, Delores turned her heavily mascara'd eyes on her.

"I thought my assistant told you to wear blue and orange."

"My skirt's blue," Cecily said, skipping the Broncos speech.

"Denim isn't quite the kind of blue we had in mind. Plus the jacket's mud-brown. You'll look like a lump of dirt." Squinting, Delores clenched the cigarette between her teeth as she reached for the jacket. "Let's take it off, dear."

Not having the stamina to take on yet another battle, Cecily shrugged out of one of her favorite Well Suited designs.

Delores draped it over her arm, her wrinkled red lips moving as she read "Get the Party Started" on Cecily's T-shirt.

"The pink is too pale, dear. It'll wash out under the lights. We have a lovely sky-blue jacket that'll

could remember. She and her mother had
deal—Cecily was excused from doing ho
she was reading, which had fueled her
and disdain for dust mops. She lov
suspense, her all-time favorite A
Jim Thompson. These days
indulge her love of readin
Patricia Cornwell in h
within forty-eight h

All Cecily n
words in the
she'd be
were
ne

he escape the dress-code police? Probably did a number twenty-three on Delores, who appeared to be the Chief of Dress-code Police, mesmerizing her into forgetting about the blue and orange policy.

She eyed Adam at the bar reading his script, his forehead creased with consternation. So, Mr Maligned wasn't too happy with the surprise story-line and suggested dialogue, either, eh?

Suddenly her bleak mood lifted.

Not just that misery loved company, but because she also sensed she had the competitive edge.

She was an avid reader, had been as long as she

had a
usework if
love of books
ed mysteries and
Hell of a Woman by
s, she was too busy to
g, although put a book by
r hands and it'd be devoured
ours.

eeded to do was pick out a few key
script, get a sense of the "flow", and
ahead of the game. So what if the writers
lueless about her and Adam's books? All she
ded to do was drop a tidbit from *The Perfect
Boyfriend* here and there. Come to think of it, that
was how she operated on her radio show. She
always knew the theme of the evening, plus whatever directions—the flow—the producer wanted the
show to take. Never stopped her from improvising,
though.

With an extra bounce to her step, Cecily almost
skipped to the canvas chair with her script. Flowing,
teleprompting, whatever, this woman could handle it.

Twenty-five grand, here I come.

Adam bit off an expletive as he flipped through the
last pages of the script.

He'd already logged a complaint with the assistant director, then with Bradley, telling both of them
that trying to nail "the flow" right before going on

the air was like changing the rules of the game right before the teams hit the field.

Screw this. He shoved the script aside.

Besides, he already had his game plan down, which was to play aggressively. Play to win. As he noted in his book and often quoted on his radio show, "Winning isn't everything, it's the only thing." One of his favorite Vince Lombardi quotes.

A spiky-headed kid with a megaphone was coaching the extras—women looking like Britney Spears, guys like Colin Farrell—on acting natural, not looking into the camera, not blocking the stars.

On the last word, heads turned and looked at him.

He nodded, smiled.

Some looked across the room at Cecily, but she was lost in her own world. Leaning back in her chair, she flipped through the script, oblivious to the movement of people and equipment around her. The woman had incredible focus. On the athletic side, too, from the look of those toned calves.

A woman like that would make a killer point guard in a basketball game.

Cecily suddenly looked up and their gazes caught.

Even from across the room, he swore he saw a spark in her eyes. Oh, man. Loved those eyes. Big, dark. Like beacons of sexuality. Went with the slightly mussed hair, like she could care if she wasn't perfectly put together. This was the kind of woman who'd look hot traipsing around in nothing but a man's shirt. Helping herself to a cup of morning coffee, or a late-night indulgence of ice cream. Just a spoon and carton, none of that Miz Manners two scoops in a bowl. Cecily would flick her tongue on the creamy confection, looking at the lucky guy with those killer eyes hooded with sleep…or lust.

Let's go for the lust.

Oh, yeah. Sex with her would be physical, rollicking, fun. The lady was creative, so toss in experimental, too.

Raking a hand through his hair, he blew out a burst of pent-up breath. Man, this was *not* the time to conjure heated thoughts about his opponent. His strategy had to remain focused on manipulating her, besting her, undermining her…

Not wanting to bed her.

But, considering the heat blasting through his veins, his best move was to make his libido work in his favor for the time being.

From across the room, she flashed him a small smile.

He grinned back, thinking how hot she'd look in his long-sleeve blue oxford…unbuttoned all the way…

He made a mental note to pick up a pint of vanilla ice cream on the way home.

CHAPTER FOUR

AN HOUR and forty minutes later, Cecily again stood inside the front door to Appetites as a technician attached a wireless microphone to the inside of her jacket. Several minutes ago, Bradley, trailed by an entourage, had positioned Cecily here, explaining the show would open with a long shot of her. She was to act as though she'd "just walked inside".

The room crackled with activity. A boom mike swayed over the bar, hangers-on sipped coffee and chatted to each other as they watched monitors, lighting techs focused yellow- and pink-tinted lights along the bar. At one of the stools sat Adam, chatting with an animated extra who looked like a Britney Spears wannabe.

The second-floor manager's office—which had a window that looked down on the main floor—had become a control booth where people with head-phones observed the action below.

The stage manager, wearing a tie-dyed shirt and

jeans, spoke through a bullhorn. "People, listen up! We're going live in twenty minutes."

Cecily gulped a breath.

"Don't pat the area over the microphone," said the technician, a barrel-shaped guy who looked to be in his thirties, "or bend your head to talk into it. Just move and speak naturally and you'll be clearly heard."

Clearly heard. By ten million strangers. Cecily nodded, praying to God she didn't burp.

"Everything okay?"

"I wish I hadn't eaten that burrito for lunch."

The technician frowned. "No, I meant the place-ment of the mike."

"Oh." She swallowed hard, wondering if that could be heard, too. "It's fine."

The technician left and Delores stepped forward.

"You'll be great, dear," she whispered while fuss-ing with the jacket. She smelled of cigarettes and White Shoulders.

"I'm shaking."

"Pre-show jitters, happens to the best of 'em. Trust me, when the cameras start rolling, you'll be fine."

"Easy for you to say."

"Might be hard to believe to look at me now…" she brushed something off a sleeve "…but back when the dinosaurs still roamed the earth, I walked the boards." She caught the question in Cecily's expres-sion. "Meaning, I was an actress."

When she smiled, Cecily saw a prettiness in Delores's features she hadn't noticed before. And for a moment she saw Delores in her youth. Heart-shaped face, bright blue eyes and, although her hair was mostly gray now, Cecily imagined it'd been auburn, heavy on the copper to match the older woman's sparky personality.

Delores shrugged. "Been in your shoes. I know how it is."

She stepped back and tilted her head as she gave Cecily a general once-over. "The blue jacket complements your hair and eyes. That other jacket dragged down your coloring, didn't do you justice."

Cecily made a mental note to check her inventory for any blue or orange Well Suited jackets. If not, she'd make one before the next date. That was, if she survived this first one.

Delores shook a cigarette out of a pack. "Take a word of advice from this old broad. Brad's a pussycat faking it as a lion. His dream is to win an Emmy, which means he'll do whatever it takes to make this show sparkle. Problem is, and he'd never admit it— male pride and all that—but he's damn uncomfortable with the whole reality-show concept. Sure, there's a five-second lapse where he can toss in one of the extras if something goes wrong—"

"Has he ever had to do that before?" Cecily cut in, her imagination reeling with the chaos that could ensue if something couldn't be fixed in five seconds.

"Maybe once or twice. Nothing major. Those extras, some of whom he brought from LA, are talented actresses and actors who can wing it on a moment's notice."

Cecily looked at the spandexed wonder fawning over Adam. Wouldn't he just love it if one of these babes suddenly had to fill in?

"Bottom line, dear, don't waste time worrying about Brad and his scripts and teleprompter. It's more for his benefit than yours. The man is terrified things won't go off perfectly, that's all."

Seemed they were all worried about something being perfect. *The Perfect Boyfriend, The Perfect Girlfriend*, this show.

"Just be yourself. That's why you're here." Delores flicked a lighter to the tip of her cigarette and took a drag as the make-up girl moved in and started dabbing at Cecily's face.

"How ya doin'?" asked the girl, snapping gum while talking. A diamond stud twinkled in her nose.

"Oh, fine," Cecily murmured as she watched Delores walk away.

Just be yourself. Which in Cecily's twenty-four years had been a given, but now seemed the strangest thing to do in front of millions of viewers.

But, like it or not, the next hour-plus was her destiny. She had to do it to make her future work. Even if she had the sudden, irrational urge to just walk out and leave this Hollyweirdness, she couldn't. As Adam had so nicely put it, she'd be sued. *For anything and everything and some his people would make up just to piss me off.*

The stage manager raised her bullhorn. "Listen up, people!"

All the scraping and chatting subsided.

"We're fifteen minutes to going live!"

It was almost time to face her destiny.

Nearly fifteen minutes later, Bradley, positioned high on his director's chair, scanned the room with an imperial air.

"Ladies and gentleman," he began, his mellow baritone carrying across the hushed bar, "we're almost down to the count. Remember, ignore the cameras, don't gawk at the principals, act natural. And most important—have fun!"

He nodded to the stage manager, whose headset was nearly lost in the mass of golden-red curls on her head.

"Anybody who hasn't ditched their cell or pager," she announced loudly, "do so now."

An extra tossed his to a production assistant.

All eyes were on the stage manager as she looked up at the control booth. She held up her hand, fingers spread wide.

"And we're five…" she closed her thumb so four fingers were raised "….four…three…two…"

On one, she went silent, holding up her index finger before pointing at Cecily.

Adam, perched on a stool at the bar, experienced a wild surge of adrenalin. Everything he'd worked toward this last year—the self-publishing and distribution of his book, the word of mouth that had grown into his own radio spot, his name on the verge of being known nationwide—came to fruition at this very moment.

The overhead lights warmed his skin. The energy in the room was so intense, he had the sense he could reach out and touch it.

All eyes were on Cecily who stood in front of the door, staring into a camera with a deer-in-the-headlights look.

A few seconds passed…each feeling like a small eternity.

He could almost hear the cumulative breath held by every single person as they waited for Cecily to do *something*. The extras kept up their quiet banter as though nothing were out of the ordinary and this were a real bar, although Adam caught Bradley pointing at one of them, ready to give the order for her to jump in.

Suddenly, he felt the urge to protect Cecily. Nobody deserved to fall flat on her face before she'd even had a chance. Adam, former high-school quarterback, knew how to think on his feet when a game was in jeopardy.

Clearing his throat to get Bradley's attention, Adam made a great show of standing. It got the director's attention.

A camera swerved, focused on Adam.

"Babe," he called out, holding his arms open wide, "come to your Stud Man!"

Her stunned look morphed into a peeved one. *Exactly* the reaction he'd expected.

"My name's Cecily," she said tightly.

"And a beautiful name it is, too," Adam said, strolling toward her.

He crossed the space in several large strides and gave her a light, sideways hug. That familiar floral scent wafted up to greet him.

Taking her by the elbow, he steered her to their seats at the bar. She walked stiffly, which he guessed was part of her nervousness, although he could tell by the flash in her eyes that he'd ignited her ire.

Which was, of course, exactly what he wanted. They were opponents, after all. Wouldn't be an entertaining show if she didn't kick off the game being thoroughly pissed off at his—what had she called them?—*maladjusted* ways.

From the corner of his eye, he saw Bradley lean back in his chair, clutching his heart as though he'd barely avoided a heart attack. The woman running the boom mike panned back.

"Great spot, isn't it?" Adam said, making a big display of helping Cecily onto the stool. As she settled in he left his hand on her back a bit longer than necessary in full view of the camera.

Dating rule number eight. On a first date—or as we studs call it, a *priming* date—touch her at least five times. Casual, unassuming touches that set the pace for more intimate touches later.

"Appetites is one of Denver's hottest spots," he continued, easing onto his seat next to her. This was part of the program, starting off the show with some free PR for Appetites.

Cecily nodded, cleared her throat. "I've heard it has the biggest offering of micro-brewed beers in the region…"

Good. She was relaxing.

"…Colorado has more micro-breweries per square mile than…"

Relaxing and talking. *A lot.*

Adam glanced at the teleprompter. Damn if she wasn't reading this off, word for word, in a near-monotone. If he didn't do something, she'd sit and read those slowly scrolling words for the rest of the date and put everyone to sleep.

"Hey," he whispered, touching his finger to her chin and turning her face gently so their gazes met.

Touch number two. Let the hand linger.

But even as he acted out his priming-date basics for the guys in the audience to see, he was overly aware of the silkiness of her skin. How her chest rose and fell in quickened breaths.

Lightly gripping her chin with his thumb and forefinger—mostly to keep her in place so she wasn't tempted to read the teleprompter again—he said, "Let's not forget my bar, Home Plate, has a great selection of home brews, too. Plus an entertainment room filled with billiard tables, dartboards, video games and wall-mounted screens for sports viewing."

Her pretty mouth thinned with annoyance.

"So, uh, what kind of sports do you like?" he asked, dropping his hand.

"Anything that doesn't include brats."

He laughed. "Touché. No team sports?"

"I'll watch a Broncos game now and then. But as to what *I* enjoy doing, that'd be designing clothes." She turned and looked at the camera. "Especially," she said with a smile, "Well Suited jackets, my line of urban-fem wear for the woman who knows who she is."

Bradley gestured madly at the teleprompter, which Cecily ignored.

"If you want to know more, check out *www.urban-femwear.com*," she continued, "and ask about my new customer discount. Remember, that's Well Suited jackets, for the woman who knows who she is."

She looked back at Adam, a conspiratorial glint in her eye. She might have been frozen at first, but she was warming up, fast.

In some ways, they weren't at such opposite ends of the spectrum, he realized. They were both entrepreneurs, determined to promote themselves and their businesses. He didn't know a lot about Well Suited, but, from her scrappy personality, he'd guess she'd started her business from scratch, the same way he'd started Home Plate.

That took toughness. And a lot of guts.

Bradley was gesturing madly at his misbehaving, self-promoting stars.

Before they moved on to another subject, however, Adam needed to prompt Cecily to clarify something for her potential customers.

"Is this," he said, lightly touching the lapels, "one of your Well Suited jackets?"

"God, no!"

A techie laughed out loud, them promptly shut up.

"Sorry, Delores," she murmured under her breath.

"Well, the color is a good choice," Adam said. "It brings out your eyes."

He brushed back a curl of hair as though to see her eyes better, knowing the dudes in the audience were chalking up touch number three. Yeah, ol' Adam might be admiring of his opponent, even willing to help her pitch her product, but this was still all about winning and he fully intended to get the most votes after this date.

As he curled a lock around his finger he winked at her.

Rule number eleven. Winking at a babe creates a moment of intimacy between the two of you. This wink is fast, fleeting…don't treat it like a garage door lowering. Combine it with one of the five priming-date touches and you're first and ten, on your way to a touchdown.

She blinked back, and he caught a look of such utter guilelessness in her face that he momentarily felt ashamed for manipulating her so blatantly.

He raised his free hand, thinking to touch her reassuringly—screw whatever number it was—when she shifted a little. He wasn't sure exactly what happened next, but somehow their fingertips touched and heated lightning jumped between them. Hot, sizzling.

From the startled sound she made, she felt it, too.

He tore his gaze from her eyes and stared, dumbfounded, at their hands, amazed at how a simple touch had just rocked his world. Sure, he'd touched her before now, but that had been *him* touching *her,* not the two of them connecting. As much as he hated to think it, connecting as equals.

He sat there and stared at his large brown fingers intertwined with the small white ones of this irritating, opinionated, exciting woman who was driving him more than a little crazy.

"What'll it be?" A bartender materialized and slid coasters in front of them.

With great effort, Adam turned his gaze to the man, undoubtedly one of the extras cued by Bradley to interrupt the stunned silence that had suddenly engulfed Cecily and Adam.

Adam cleared his throat. "What do you have on tap?"

The bartender rattled off some beers, and Adam ordered a Fat Tire. As Cecily ordered a margarita Adam gave himself a mental wake-up call.

You just benched yourself, buddy. Time to get back into the game.

As the bartender sauntered away Adam eased his hand away from Cecily's.

Next time he touched her, he'd keep his wits about him.

Minutes later—ten, fifteen?—Cecily took another sip of her margarita, damn glad it had a bit of alcohol because what she needed right now was to relax, not worry. Miraculously, the cameras were still rolling, Bradley wasn't freaking out—well, much—and she and Adam were doing their best to take their cues from the teleprompter.

Although, in the back of her mind, she still hadn't fully recovered from that zap of steamy-needy-whoa-baby heat that had transpired between her and Adam. She'd been prepared to deal with his advances. After all, the man laid out his "primer date" philosophy, and that smarmy five-touch rule, with great detail in his book.

She'd even been somewhat prepared for his taking her side and helping her promote her Well Suited business. She could almost quote verbatim his reasoning for that from his book—*Act interested in the babe, even take her side, and she'll be not only flattered, but indebted.*

Right, *indebted.* As though a woman might, like, owe the guy something later?

But a whole new game had kicked in when her and Adam's fingertips had accidentally touched.

She still wasn't sure what had happened. All she

knew was suddenly something had turned molten between them. Something scorching and powerful. It had kindled pinpoints of desire in his eyes. Made her breaths grow ragged.

The *last* thing she'd expected to experience with *Adam.*

And it had happened in front of millions of viewers.

Looking back, she wasn't sure how long it had lasted. Seconds? Minutes?

It had ended when that bartender had appeared and broken the spell. After ordering their drinks, she and Adam had bumbled through some chit-chat, taking turns reading right off the teleprompter. Bradley had made gestures, even held up a sign that said in big bold letters "Will you two get it together," which would have made Cecily laugh if she hadn't been so freaked out about what had transpired.

Electricity with Stud Man? Megan was probably on her knees in front of the TV, praying for Cecily's soul.

Now here they were ten or fifteen minutes later, starting to act normal again, whatever that was.

"Ever hear of the Capital Asset Pricing Model?"

"Huh?" She scanned the teleprompter, not recalling this piece of flow.

Suddenly, she was hearing words like "asset pricing", "interest rates" and "market efficiency". It was worse than the time she'd been on a blind date with that CPA, who'd darn near put her to sleep with his monologue on the tax benefits of an S Corporation. She'd finally excused herself to go to the bathroom, then never returned.

Obviously, something she couldn't do in the middle of *Marriage Material...or Misfortune?*

Cecily touched Adam's arm. "Uh, excuse me."

He paused, blinked.

"What are you talking about?"

"My finance studies at Duke University. Figured as we're both business owners, you'd be interested."

"I like numbers, yes. I also like mysteries, but that doesn't mean I can spend hours talking about autopsy reports."

With barely a pause, Adam picked up where he'd left off. "The systematic risk cannot be diversified away. On the other hand, an *unsystematic* risk..."

She glanced at the clock. *My, how time flies when you're not having fun.* Amazingly, their date was going to be over in ten minutes.

Panic flooded her.

Because she'd done next to zilch using her book rules to gain the advantage.

Adam, on the other hand, had railroaded numerous items from his own book while, at the same time, annihilating several of hers. Such as, at this very moment, stomping on her and Megan's rule about the perfect boyfriend being a great listener.

"...with applications to market microstructure..."

Plus, while droning on about the most boring stuff on the planet and not letting her get a word in edgewise, he was ogling every Saran-wrapped extra who sashayed past. Which seemed to be a non-stop stream as the "babes" realized they had only a few precious minutes to get some camera time before the show ended.

Which clearly attacked her rule that the perfect boyfriend never window-shopped while with his date.

Adam paused to check out a black-leather mini-skirt with fishnet stockinged legs.

Cecily mentally scrambled for a vote-winning move. *Quick, think of some of your and Megan's favorite rules.*

Number three. The Perfect Boyfriend *loves* me in sweatpants.

Right. Like that had anything to do with her nun-like denim skirt and the spandexed babes draped all over the bar.

Number five. The Perfect Boyfriend laughs at my jokes.

Normally, that one had great possibilities…except if the guy was yammering on about things like dynamic economic models and market efficiency. Real easy to slip in a joke there. *Not.*

Number four. The Perfect Boyfriend has an Australian accent.

If Cecily remembered correctly, she and Megan had been deep into their third margaritas and a heavy-duty Hugh Jackman fantasy when they'd come up with that one.

She glanced at the clock again. Almost down to the wire.

On the teleprompter, she caught the word "juke-box".

Right! This was one of the flows: to go to the jukebox, reminisce about favorite tunes and pick out one together. Hey, piece of cake—once there, checking out tune titles, some word would trigger one of her rules and the rest would be chump change.

She stood up, holding her drink. "Let's check out some tunes."

She didn't wait for Adam to agree. Darn near jogging, she headed a few feet to the jukebox. Reaching it, she turned. Sure enough, a camera was following her.

And so was Adam.

He reached her and set his beer down on a side table.

Over his shoulder, she eyed the clock. Less than three minutes to make a play for her side.

The thought broke apart as Adam suddenly took her by surprise, pulling her into a full body embrace. He looked down at her, his blue eyes narrowed and intense, his rugged face bathed in warm yellows and pinks from the overhead lights.

Seemed Adam wasn't wasting time, either.

He was going for a last-minute big play, although

she didn't remember anywhere in his book where coming on like a gorilla in heat was a way to woo the perfect girlfriend. In fact, didn't he say in his book that the first frontal hug should be short to gauge a woman's response, sense her readiness?

Not that Cecily was born yesterday. She could handle an awkward pass.

But when he grabbed her butt with a full-handed basketball-grip and squeezed, she lost it.

Furious, she grabbed his sweater with her free hand. Stretching up on her tiptoes, she jerked him closer until his nose came down almost on a level with hers.

"Listen, you gorilla," she said into his face. "I'm going to tell you something and you had better listen real good because if I have to repeat it again, all deals are off."

She looked past Adam's head at Bradley, who stared back wide-eyed, before swerving her gaze to the wall clock.

Less than a minute to go.

She met Adam's shocked stare again.

"Just because we had a moment of electricity doesn't mean you have the right to monkey wrestle me, got it?"

"But—"

"Or grab my butt."

Adam slowly straightened, breaking her grip on his sweater. When he stood to his full height, she realized the top of her head could fit neatly underneath his chin.

But this was an issue about dominance, not size or strength.

"Since you're a finance kinda guy," she said, knowing the mike was picking up her every single word, "perhaps next time you consider hustling a woman, consider the effects of cold-cash flow."

Adam gasped as she poured the rest of her margarita down the front of his pants.

"And…cut!" yelled Bradley.

"Cut," yelled the stage manager.

"Cut," yelled Roger.

"Cut," murmured Cecily to Adam before she sauntered away.

CHAPTER FIVE

"So what if he grabbed your butt like a basketball? Sweetpea, that riled-up response of yours was better than…" Theodore stirred his double-mocha-caramel-something drink while he thought for a moment. Suddenly, he snapped his fingers. "Renée Zellweger!"

"Renée Zellweger?"

"You know, like in *Bridget Jones's Diary.*"

"I knew I should have gone on a diet before starting that dating-from-hell show." She stared at her half-eaten maple scone. "Bridget Jones. Wonderful."

"Wonderful's right. That woman nailed both Hugh Grant and Colin Firth." Theodore waggled his eyebrows over the rim of his cup as he took a sip.

He set down his cup. "Forget Bridget Jones. Renée Zellweger in *Jerry Maguire*, then. Or *Cold Mountain.*" He held up his hand as Cecily started to speak. "I know what you're going to say. No, that blue jacket didn't make you look like her in that movie!"

He leaned forward slightly, and she caught a whiff of his cologne, a touch of pine needle, a bit of cinnamon. Gay men were so good with seasonal touches.

"Speaking of jackets," he said, "what do you think of mine?"

She reached out and touched it. The world could be crashing around them, but there was always time to stop and discuss clothes. Especially jackets.

"Soft," she said, rubbing her fingers on the material. "But not suede."

"Brushed microfiber. Machine-washable."

"Like the color."

"Brown's the new black, you know."

He patted the numerous pockets, then blinked his hazel eyes at her. "Are we over the *Cold Mountain* reference?"

"Somewhat."

"I'm not going to name any more movies. All I'm saying is Renée is hot and cute when she gets worked up, and that was *so* you last night."

"Hot and cute," Cecily muttered, rolling her eyes.

"As your almost-best friend, may I say you're being overly sensitive about this. Last night, you overcame a less-than-stellar entrance to a dramatic grand finale that won you eighty percent of the vote! So what if the man grabbed your butt? You won! Which just goes to prove that old adage, there's no such thing as bad PR."

Which Theodore had said multiple times since he and Cecily had met to debrief at his favorite Starbucks downtown. He'd called first thing this morning with the news she'd won and to get her butt-grabbed self out to celebrate.

Cecily took a sip of her latte, welcoming the warm rush of milk and caffeine. It almost—not quite, but almost—soothed her edgy nerves. But then, nothing short of going into the FBI's witness relocation program could repair her embarrassment over last night's date.

"Even my *grandmother* saw that," she murmured.

"We're back to the butt?"

Cecily flashed Theodore a look. "If you'd had your behind grabbed in front of millions of strangers… Oh, never mind." He would have loved it.

From the glint in Theodore's eyes, he'd obviously just read her thought. "Gay men are notorious exhibitionists—what can I say? By the way, all my friends voted for you."

"They voted for *me* over *Adam*?" She grinned. "I'm honored."

"Well, I didn't say it was an easy choice," he teased. "Seriously, Adam may have acted like a beast at the end of the show, but he did some very gallant things prior to that. Remember, girlfriend, when the show started with a close-up of you looking like someone had zapped you with Freon, that hunk of male came to the rescue. And when you did that oh-so-persuasive plug for your Well Suited jackets, he made sure it was clear that godawful Tums-blue number you were wearing wasn't one of your designs."

Cecily groaned, slugged down another sip of latte as she glanced at sections of *The Denver Post* newspaper scattered on another table. One of the smaller headlines read Beauty Battled and Won!

Amazing how public an introverted girl's life could get.

A twenty-something guy strolled into the coffee shop, snagging Theodore's attention. The two men exchanged a glance before Theodore returned his gaze to Cecily.

"I so love that 'designer black leather jacket over distressed jeans' look," he whispered, referring to the guy. "But back to you. I bet every man and woman between the ages of eight and eighty swooned at that very moment of your and Adam's meltdown."

Cecily took a long sip of her drink. Whenever she thought about that moment when they had touched, her fingers tingled all over again.

Adam's imprint had stayed with her, as though pressed onto her psyche. As she'd walked down the Sixteenth Street Mall to meet Theodore this morning, uninvited images of Adam had surfaced in her mind. The wide, full shape of his lips. His cocky, commanding presence. And even though she'd never admit she'd looked, the man could fill a pair of pants.

She had tried to shake those thoughts, and others, but it was as though he'd infiltrated her mind. Like some kind of sensual spyware, steamy images of him popped up unexpectedly to tease her.

Those mental pictures wouldn't be occurring, however, if Adam hadn't apologized for that butt-grabbing moment. The viewing audience had missed his reaction after the tape had stopped rolling, when he'd realized what an idiotic move he'd made. She'd been furious, but only a heart of stone wouldn't have forgiven a man darn near on his knees begging forgiveness.

Theodore looked back at Cecily. "He wants me."

She frowned. "Adam?"

"No, silly. That boy in the black jacket. The one ordering a chai."

Cecily glanced over in time to see the guy smiling at Theodore. "Of course he wants you. You're hot and cute."

"I am, aren't I?" Theodore laughed, gave a dramatic toss of his head. "Renée Zellweger, step aside!"

He turned over the receipt for their drinks. "Got a pen? I'm jotting down my phone number for chai-boy."

"Sure." She rummaged in her handbag, pulled one out.

Theodore jotted down his number. "So, where's your next date?"

"Don't know. They're all mystery dates. Wardrobe tells me what to wear—and to make it blue and orange—then a driver picks me up the early evening of the show and takes me there."

"Blue and orange?" Theodore did a small cheerleading wave. "Well, go Broncos!" He handed back the pen and stood. "How do I look?"

"You make me want to wear microfiber."

"I love it when you talk dirty," he murmured, walking away with the strip of paper in his hand.

As Cecily watched him cross the room and slip

the piece of paper to the cute guy she wished her dating rituals were so simple.

"Gorilla Man!" called out Rodney as he strolled into Home Plate at five-thirty that night.

Adam, who'd been stocking glasses, winced. Well, that had to be expected. Grabbing Cecily's bottom last night made Neanderthals look sophisticated.

"Bad strategy—what can I say?"

"Look on the bright side. Maybe the Nuggets will make you an offer to play second string." With a loud guffaw, Rodney straddled his favorite stool.

"Very funny. Your usual?"

"Yep." He helped himself to a handful of peanuts from one of the snack bowls that dotted the bar.

The front door swung open and in sauntered Tom with his perennial hangdog expression. "Good evening, gentlemen."

"Tom, my man," said Rodney.

"How's the legal life?" asked Adam, pouring beer from a tap.

"Judge not lest ye be the judge." Tom took off his charcoal wool overcoat and folded it neatly over the back of a stool. "Speaking of the legal life, Adam, has that *Perfect Boyfriend* woman slapped you with a sexual harassment suit yet?"

"I apologized to her over ten times after the show," he said, setting the beer in front of Rodney, "and she accepted at least three of those, so I think things are okay between us."

Tom folded his hands in front of him. "A word of advice, my friend," he said somberly. "Next time you get a wild hair to do something questionable, don't. At the very least, don't do it so that it's documented on video."

"Or in front of millions of eye witnesses," added Vince loudly as he sauntered into the bar. He slapped Tom and Rodney on their backs before sitting down. "Gotta hand it to you, Adam," he said, loosening his tie, "you sure know how to impress the ladies."

Laughter.

Adam held both hands up in surrender. "I wanted to play an aggressive game. It backfired." He cringed. "No, I didn't mean it *like* that." He squirted some seltzer into a highball glass. "Tonight's our competing radio shows and I know I'm going to be trounced by the ladies."

"Maybe you should try calling them 'women'," offered Tom.

Rodney wiped some foam off his lip. "Our Stud Man? If he doesn't lead our cause, who will?"

Larry entered, punching something into his PalmPilot as he headed for the seat next to Rodney. "If you expunge the gorilla tactics, Adam, I believe you could win back the thirty-five percent of the audience you alienated last night."

"Gee, you guys really know how to cheer me up."

"Adam, bro, we're on your side," said Vince. "We're offering advice because we need you to win the next date, man. MacGruder's Marauders is at stake!"

"Here, here!"

"Go, Stud Man!"

"Beers, brats and babes!"

"Do you think," Adam said, dropping a wedge of lime into the drink before handing it to Tom, "it's too late to change that to Beer, brats and women?"

The guys laughed and joked, not realizing that Adam was partially serious. He had a plan for softening his position, playing it smarter on the next date.

Cecily would be either too stunned or too charmed to realize Adam was not only gaining on her, but taking the lead.

Six days later, at six p.m. sharp, Cecily stubbed out her third chain-smoked cigarette before she walked into the Denver Botanic Gardens.

She was anxious for the usual ten million reasons, and just a tad more because no script had been delivered to her apartment yesterday, or at the very least this morning, *as promised.* Now she was walking into *Marriage Material…or Misfortune?* totally unprepared, again, for the flow.

Hundreds of twinkling lights, mimicking the stars overhead, illuminated the plants and trees. Along the snow-shoveled walking paths were a few costumed groups of bell choirs and carolers practicing. People in coats and mufflers stood at snack stands where the scents of hot cocoa and spiced cider wafted into the air.

Really, all of this would be perfect if it weren't for the *Marriage Material…Or Misfortune?* crew

milling around. As she walked closer she saw technicians adjusting lights, cameramen positioning
their equipment and, in the midst of everything,
Bradley giving instructions to a bearded man in a
knitted cap.

Bradley spied her, waved, and headed over.

"Felicity, darling!" he enthused, wrapped in what
looked like a black raccoon coat with matching hat.

"Cecily," she murmured as they air-kissed. "I, uh,
never received a script."

He made an exaggerated pout. "Sorry, darling, we
really thought it would be ready before now."

"That's what Roger said this morning." And every
half-hour she'd called him after that.

"He'll bring it to you right away."

Great. She'd be studying the flow at the last
minute again. Not that she wasn't a quick study, but
it was stressful enough getting dressed and showing
up for these televised dates without having to do a
fast study at the last minute, too.

Bradley obviously caught her look of worry
because he patted her arm reassuringly. "The flow
will be on the teleprompter. Not to worry, darling."
He clapped his hands. "Take off your coat, Felicity,
let's see how you look."

"Ceci— Oh, never mind." She pulled off her long
black winter coat.

Bradley's smile dropped. He pointed to one of his
entourage. "Go get Delores. *Now.*"

* * *

Two hours later, wearing more make-up than a cadaver and a duck-down orange coat that made her look like The Return of the Great Pumpkin, a dangerously-approaching-the-edge Cecily watched the stage manager—whom she discovered everyone called Sugar Megs—raise the bullhorn to her mouth.

"Anybody who hasn't ditched their cell or pager, do it now."

As several extras tossed their cells Cecily wished she could ditch something, too. Like herself. Over a cliff.

Adam was a no-show.

And Bradley had insisted the show go on, with her alone.

Cecily had asked if one of the extras—one of those Colin Farrell wannabes—could at least fill in so she wasn't suddenly starring in the Cecily Cassell Gets Stood Up show.

But, no, Bradley had insisted he wanted just her, fuming and seething as she'd been doing ever since Roger, the perennial bearer of good news, had whispered to Cecily to *please* not freak out, but Adam was nowhere to be found.

She'd tried to not openly show her emotions, but that wasn't her style. She'd never been terribly adept hiding how she really felt. And she felt damn angry that Adam had the audacity to stand her up on their second date, leaving her to wing it solo in front of millions of viewers.

When she'd asked Bradley if that meant she won

by default, he'd laughed, muttered something like, "Read the clause in your contract."

If worst came to worst, he'd said reassuringly, he'd always bring in an extra. Or they might pan to the carolers as they broke into song.

Oh, lovely. Cecily could see it now. Her standing frozen, staring into the camera as a chorus of heavenly voices boomed "Hallelujah!"

Sugar Megs, her golden-red curls peeking from underneath a beanie cap over which she'd stuck her headset, held up her hand, fingers spread wide. "And we're five…"

"Bradley?" Cecily said tightly.

"Four…"

"What?"

"Three…"

"Can we discuss the choice of songs the carolers might suddenly start booming—?"

Too late. Sugar Megs turned silent, held up her index finger for "one", then pointed to Cecily.

Who stared at the camera, figuring she must have really screwed up in a past life considering her current karma.

Bradley was making that rolling "get going, get going!" motion with his hands.

"Greetings, viewers," she said quickly, the mist from her breath rising into the night air.

Good. No rousing chorus of Handel's *Messiah*.

Yet.

"Tonight's *Marriage Material…or Misfortune?*

stars me, Cecily Cassell, all by myself because Adam the Stud Man MacGruder decided to stand me up. If this were real life, I'd be about ready to leave because one of *The Perfect Boyfriend* rules is that a woman *never* waits over fifteen minutes for a guy."

Bradley pointed frantically at the teleprompter.

Oh, right, during her rapid skim of the script flow she'd read how the show was to kick off with her plugging tonight's location.

"We're taping live from the Denver Botanic Gardens," she read, "and their annual Blossoms of Light with over nine hundred thousand lights throughout seventeen acres of gardens. Point to tree."

She heard Bradley groan.

"Oh. Sorry." She pointed to the tree she stood in front of, its branches twinkling with a constellation of white and gold lights. When she looked back for the teleprompter, some guy in a red jacket blocked it.

"So this tree…"

Tree. Tree. She knew nothing about trees! If only she'd paid closer attention in her biology classes. Or was that botany?

"So this tree…is my date tonight, it appears."

Somebody shoved the guy out of the way, who slid a little on some ice as he caught his balance.

"But then, girls," she said companionably, fighting the urge to laugh. This wasn't so bad. If she could wing it on radio, heck, she could wing it now. "Let's face it. A tree's better than a man because…"

She walked over to the tree and patted its trunk with one of her orange-mittened hands.

"It's grounded, for starters."

One of the techies snorted.

"And because…" she thought of Megan and that horrendous dating experience, where the guy had asked her to dress in leather and go to a swingers club, the request that had kicked off their infamous night of margaritas and their penning *The Perfect Boyfriend* "…because the only swinging it'll ask you to do is from its branches."

Hey, this was starting to be fun.

"Let's see," she said, her boots crunching in the snow as she walked around the tree. In her peripheral vision, she caught Bradley's anguished hand gestures.

She gave him a little wave back.

"A tree is also better than a man because it doesn't dominate the conversation, doesn't make you lug a puce-colored couch all the way across country only to fool around on you, and sometimes a tree even grows its own flowers—"

"Sorry I'm late," interrupted a familiar male voice.

She turned.

There stood Adam, looking sheepish and way too handsome, holding out a bouquet of red roses. He was heaving breaths, and she realized he must have run onto the set.

"The driver took a side trip to avoid a traffic jam and got lost." He dragged a hand through his tousled hair. "Sorry."

"And trees don't show up late with lame excuses."

"I mean it," he said, sounding so sincere she could almost hear women swooning in television-land. "I'm sorry."

He wore a black wool topcoat, partially unbuttoned to reveal a gray-blue cashmere turtleneck that brought out his killer-blue eyes. Add his mussed hair, and that chagrined smile, and he was looking a hell of a lot better than, say, a mighty oak.

She accepted the flowers, their sweet scent mingling with traces of cider.

"Thank you."

"You're welcome." A smile slow-danced across his face. "You look lovely tonight."

She smiled back as a dizzying current raced through her. *Oh, no. Don't go there.* She quickly glanced down at her orange down coat, which had puffed out slightly with her body heat.

"I look like a walking pumpkin."

He gave his head a shake. "Women and their self-images."

Followed instantly by a wait-a-minute movement with his hand at the camera.

"I didn't mean it in a bad way, ladies! I just mean society has imposed such unrealistic expectations on how you're supposed to look, as though something's wrong if you don't look like Cindy Crawford—well, no wonder you're sometimes overly hard on yourselves."

Cecily realized her mouth was open but couldn't have shut it if she tried.

He looked back at her. "Something wrong?"

"I'm going to check the basement for pods."

He laughed heartily, then stepped closer and looked warmly at her. "Don't worry about the jacket. Anyway, orange becomes you."

Their gazes held, and for a moment the world seemed different. The air was softer, the twinkling lights brighter, each passing moment more alive.

"Cecily…"

The sound of his voice caused a tremor to run through her body.

"Huh?"

"You all right?"

He touched her lightly on the arm, and she swore she felt his heat all the way to her skin. It was hard to think. Her thoughts exploded into tiny flames that danced in her head.

Vaguely, she became aware of Bradley gesturing, Sugar Megs pacing, the rustling of the carolers…

As though awoken abruptly from a dream, she jerked her gaze to the teleprompter, ready to glom onto any string of words before "Hallelujah" boomed.

Something about balls of mistletoe…

Mistletoe?

No way she was getting into a situation where they were supposed to kiss. If she fell into a stupor over a mere touch, God help her if their lips touched.

"Shall we look at the Japanese Garden?" she said

cheerily. In her last-minute script-skimming, she recalled something written about such a garden nearby.

Adam blinked, obviously taken aback at her abrupt about-face.

"Sure," he said, glancing at the teleprompter, "after we check out the balls of mistletoe."

No, this wouldn't do. Things had gone too far. Whatever had happened a few moments ago needed to stay there, in their immediate past. She didn't need to get into a situation where she and Adam co-mingled breaths. He was the *Stud Man,* for God's sake. What was wrong with her?

"This is our second date," she said pointedly.

"Yes, I know."

"I prefer to take it easy on the first few dates, get to know someone, not..."

"Not what?"

"You know."

"Remind me."

The dog. Making her say it.

"I don't believe there's any rush to...get intimate," she said quietly.

He did a double take that was worthy of a silent-film actor. Oh, what a ham.

"Get *intimate*?" he repeated, as though he'd never heard the word before. "Cecily," he murmured, leaning closer, his voice taking on that it's-just-between-you-and-me-babe tone.

Yeah, you and me and ten million others.

"After the last date where I blew it with that basketball grip, there's no way I want to make an inappropriate move again."

Oh, he was good. Well, she'd counteract that one.

"What about your rule that the perfect girlfriend puts out on date one?"

"Well, any guy will tell you that making love to a beautiful woman on a first or even second date is a perfect *fantasy*. Sure I played on that in my book, but the truth is I'd rather be sensitive to the woman's time-table. Be intimate when *she's* ready to be intimate."

You rat. Quoting from my own book! Now she got his game plan. Instead of pitting *his* rules against hers, he was cozying up to her rules. Massaging them, using them, damn near making love to them.

If Stud Man wanted to play war of the words, she was game.

Cecily glared at him over the roses. *Bring it on, baby.*

CHAPTER SIX

"WELL," said Adam, giving Cecily his best meaning-ful look, "any guy will tell you that making love to a beautiful woman on a first or even second date is a perfect *fantasy*. Sure, I played on that in my book, but the truth is I'd rather be sensitive to the woman's time-table. Be intimate when *she's* ready to be intimate."

Man, she's eating this up. Like spoon-feeding vanilla ice cream to a shirt-clad babe.

Tonight, his game plan was to keep her off balance. He'd blown date one in this game, and he was doing a full-court press to get it back. And not by the testosterone tactics viewers expected, but by stealing a maneuver or two from the "Ten Magnetic Males" chapter in his book, number six being *"The Sensitive New-Age Guy (SNAG)"*.

How to SNAG her. Women dig it when you're nice, helpful and sensitive to her issues. Which is all well and good, just don't forget that un-derneath the act you're still a *guy*. Go easy on the crystals, long hair and playing the acoustic guitar in the woods. If you're starting to feel like you're all light and goodness, get more guy friends and eat more meat.

Cecily's eyes narrowed. "Nice try, stealing a quote from my book, but since when do *you* care about a woman's timetable?"

He leaned closer, taking in her sweet perfume. "Would you believe, since I met you?"

"No."

"How about, since I realized behaving like a Neanderthal wasn't going to win your favor."

"You mean, since you realized behaving like a Neanderthal wouldn't help you win votes."

"How about we're both right?" He smiled.

She didn't.

He cleared his throat. "Seriously, tonight I'm using some of the gentler approaches in my book." When she started to speak, he held up his hand. "I know. From a feminist perspective, my book makes me sound like I'm telling guys to be total jerks, but that's not the case."

She made a snorting noise. "You wouldn't recognize a feminist if she grabbed *you* in the ass."

He knew better than to take a side trip down the feminism highway where he'd be lucky if the worst he got was a speeding ticket.

He glanced over at Bradley, who had a what-the-hell-are-you-doing? look on his face.

If Adam was throwing off Cecily *and* the director, millions of viewers were feeling the same way. Which was a good thing. To quote from his book, "Surprises are good because if you capture a woman's imagination and mind, you'll capture the rest, too."

"Cecily," Adam said, swerving his gaze back to her, "we're quibbling over the meaning of words, which you and I both know are in themselves empty." He gestured toward the teleprompter. "Like the words they want us to parrot for this show. They're just words."

Bradley coughed.

"So," Adam continued, "are we agreed, words can be deceiving?"

"Only if they're stolen and misused—"

"Because if we agree words are deceiving, then what matters most is action." He lowered his voice, going in for the hoop shot. "Because what you have before you, Cecily, is a man who felt like a jerk after the last date and brought you flowers to make amends. You see, I'm a caring guy, too. Believe me when I tell you I respect a woman's timetable."

She gave him a look probably meant to be critical, but he caught a flash of something else in it, too. Dared he think, a touch of sanction? Perfect. He could almost hear the votes rolling in for Adam, Stud Man of the Universe.

"Oh-h-h," she finally said, her breath escaping in a plume of white vapor, "so *that's* where all this was going. You want me to think you're a *sensitive* guy."

"Hey, because I am."

She observed him with an amused look. "Well, if it gets too much for you, just eat meat and hang out with more guys."

He paused. "You've read my book."

"Know your enemy."

"'If you know the enemy *and* know yourself, you need not fear the result of a hundred battles.'"

Her brows pressed together. "That's not from your book."

"No, *The Art of War* by Sun Tzu."

"Figures," she muttered. "So you think I don't know myself?" she asked, raising her voice. "How about you? Do you know *yourself* well enough?"

He opened his mouth, but decided it might be wiser to keep it shut. He'd always prided himself on being a rolling stone. He liked to keep moving, keep experiencing something new. Especially when it came to women.

But being forced to interact with Cecily on these shows, he had no choice but to stop rolling and stay focused on one lady. Which, like this very moment, could feel damn uncomfortable because his guard was slipping. If it slipped too much, he didn't know what he'd reveal.

All right, dammit, he didn't know himself well enough.

Cecily caught the shift in his mood because her eyes, which had been sparkling with the love of combat, suddenly flickered with curiosity, maybe a touch of concern. And if *she* recognized his vulnerable moment, so did millions of others.

Seemed his own dude self was having a surprise.

As thoughts slammed around his head he became aware of a light flurry of snowflakes dancing around them. A speck of white landed on a dark, curly lock of Cecily's hair. Another, on her pinkened cheek.

He flashed on the memory of a snow globe of his mother's, one of many his father had bought her because she loved collecting them. It contained some figures, dancing. When the globe was shaken, its interior world turned white, obscuring the couple. After a few moments, the flakes quieted and the characters were visible again.

It was as though he and Cecily were within a globe, their world shaken up. And after things quieted, what would they see?

He had the gnawing suspicion part of the answer depended on his knowing himself.

"Folks," Bradley suddenly announced, "we just cut to commercial. Take five."

"Cut," yelled Sugar Megs.

"Cut, cut," yelled several technicians, as though nobody was ever sure where fantasy ended and reality really began.

A few moments later, Delores brushed off Cecily's coat while the make-up artist and hairstylist dabbed at her face and hair.

"Don't know why you're all bothering to clean me

up when more snow will fall on me after the cameras roll again."

"Brad checked the weather report and it's just a flurry, nothing heavy ahead," said Delores, the cigarette attached to her bottom lip bobbing with her words.

"Nothing heavy ahead," repeated Cecily, "except more of Adam and his manipulations."

Delores grinned. "Hit him with the roses if he gets out of hand. Seriously, gotta admire a man who knows how to make an entrance. The way he entered the scene, all out of breath and carrying those gorgeous flowers…" She shook her head, making an "mmm" sound.

Cecily watched Delores as she fussed over Cecily's outfit, wondering how many men the older woman had watched make grand entrances.

"Are you married, Delores?"

"Widowed, honey."

"Was it a good— Sorry, I shouldn't pry."

Wheels creaked as a table filled with equipment rolled by. Sugar Megs was yelling to someone about cues. A lighting technician changed the gel on a light from bright yellow to red.

Delores straightened, took a puff. "It was a great marriage," she said on a release of smoke. "Not to say it was perfect, because nothing is, but it was damn close."

Her eyes misted, and she didn't say anything for a long moment. "Sorry about the coat," she finally said, her voice a bit softer.

"Pumpkin was never my color."

"Looks good on the monitor, though. I had a lovely blue woolen number for you, but Brad nixed it. Insisted on this orange one instead."

The hairdresser gave a last touch to Cecily's hair, then left with the make-up girl.

"People, we're going live in two minutes, thirty seconds," yelled Sugar Megs. "Places, please!"

"My Well Suited jacket was blue *with* a touch of orange. I figured it'd be perfect." Cecily winced. She was starting to hate the word perfect. "I worked hard this week to design and sew it just for tonight's show."

Delores glanced over her shoulder, then turned back and whispered, "Brad thought it was too 'retro-seventies'."

"Seventies? Even if it was, so what?"

"Yes, well, maybe he had a bad disco experience or something."

"Two minutes!" yelled Sugar Megs.

"Chin up," said Delores, giving one last touch to the lapel.

Cecily held out the roses. "Will you take these someplace? I don't want to be holding them the rest of the show."

The older woman reached for them, then stopped. "Keep them, honey. For a while longer, anyway. They soften you."

Soften? Before Cecily could ask what that meant, Delores continued, "Plus it gives him a boost to see you holding them. He likes you, you know."

"Hardly."

Delores made a clucking noise. "Young people falling in love, all full of insecurities and posturing. Don't you see the way he's looking at you?"

"Please. He's the Stud Man."

But Delores was already walking away, puffing on her cigarette.

Cecily glanced down at the roses, inhaled their sweet scent. Yes, she'd noticed the way Adam looked at her, but everything was so surreal with the crew, the cameras, that damn teleprompter, Cecily wasn't really trusting *anything* she saw.

Besides, Adam played loose and fast with his book rules, doing whatever it took to gain the advantage with viewers. How could she take a guy like that seriously? No, Delores was wrong. He didn't like *her*, he liked *winning*. This was a mental game, an intellectual sparring, mind over matter, baby.

But as Adam strode toward her, looking all rugged and dark and bad in all the good ways, her traitorous body jangled with anticipation.

I should've ditched the roses during the commercial. I feel like a damn bride strolling down these walkways with Adam.

For the past some-odd minutes—ten? Fifteen? Longer?—she and Adam had been strolling along, stealing glances at the teleprompter and making occasional comments on the glittering topiaries or cascading lights.

Well, *Adam* had been making comments. Cecily was reminding herself to buy *The Art of War* as soon as possible. She could sure use some of those war tricks, or at least some heavenly intervention, to counter Adam's too-good-to-be-true Hollywood-leading-man act. Looking dapper, bringing roses, being attentive and charming and handsome while simultaneously keeping up with the teleprompter.

The dog could sure play dirty.

Off and on, such as when he gave her an irresistible grin or shot her one of those lazily seductive looks, she'd feel a part of her soften. Like a guard caught nodding off while on duty, she'd catch herself and force her mind to stay alert. If nothing else, she wanted to prove Delores wrong. This was a reality dating show pitting two rivals and nothing more. Cecily and Adam didn't like each other and were not, under any conditions, falling in love.

"Are you all right?" asked Adam, leaning over her. Light sliced behind his head, giving him a halo effect. Unbelievable. The cad had gone from sensitive to sainthood.

"Why?"

"You're awfully quiet."

"Gee, I don't think you have advice on that in your book, do you?"

He gave her a quizzical look.

"How to handle women who aren't talking. In fact, you have just the opposite. Chapter eight, I believe. 'From Roaring Lioness to Purring Kitten'.

Let me try to remember your exact words. 'Most women love to talk, talk, talk. Try to pretend you're interested because when a woman opens up, it means she has begun to view you as a potential mate'."

He winced. "Did I really write that?"

"Sudden onset of amnesia?"

"No." He placed a big hand on his black coat, drawing attention to his wide chest. "Did I do something to upset you?"

She contrived to look affronted, although images of his chest and what it looked like underneath his coat were making it difficult to stay focused on the conversation. Did he have the kind of chest hair that swirled or tapered? Molded pecs or bulging?

What had they been talking about?

"Yes," she bluffed, fairly certain the affirmative still gave her the upper hand.

He stepped forward, so close that if she tipped forward slightly their foreheads would touch. The boom mike inched closer.

"What?" he asked, his blue eyes shining with sincerity.

Man, he was one smooth operator. Going that sincere route again. "What what?"

One side of his mouth lifted in a smile. "What have I done to upset you?"

"You're too cocky," she said, her voice dropping to a whisper.

His grin widened. "I know." She didn't think it possible for him to move even closer, but he did.

"You're a bit cocky, too, you know. I think you have what they call 'short-girl syndrome'."

"I'm not short." Despite the heat crawling up the back of her neck, she forced herself to sound cool, calm, in control.

And if she believed that, she was also the Queen of Greenland.

He bent down, his lips so close she could feel the warm puffs of his breaths as he spoke. "Stand on your toes, then. Let me see how tall you are."

Their gazes locked, their breaths mingling, she raised ever so slowly on her toes, bringing her lips dangerously closer to his.

"See?" she rasped. "I'm not that short."

"No, you aren't," he acquiesced, his lips almost, almost touching hers, "but then, does size matter?"

She stayed suspended for a moment, heat racing to her cheeks, before she suddenly rocked back onto her feet. She shoved the roses closer to her face as though the flush of her skin might blend in with the roses.

Adam's blue eyes twinkled as his gaze traveled from the roses back up to her eyes. "I think we, uh, need a little refreshment after that exchange."

She nodded, trying not to think about size and unable to think of anything else. No, technically, size didn't matter, expertise did. But throw the two together, and what resulted was better than peanut butter and chocolate.

Bradley was pacing, wringing his hands.

Adam looked around, spied a snack bar. He tilted his gaze to Cecily. "Want a hot chocolate?"

Hot chocolate. Hot peanut butter.

Hot. Hot, hot, hot, hot, hot.

She was having a Bridget Jones moment, projecting her needs onto Hugh Grant or Colin Firth or Adam MacGruder…hot, hot Adam MacGruder…

Down, girl, down.

Where was her edgy, opinionated, feminist self? The woman who'd attempted to burn her ex's puce couch, penned words of liberated wisdom, counseled female callers on how to handle men? This wasn't about size or Renée Zellweger or Hugh Grant. Okay, maybe a little about Hugh Grant, but Cecily had to get her act together, *now*, and stop thinking about all the ways she could peel her body off Adam's.

I'm suffering from the stress of appearing live on television. Yes, that was it. Spikes of adrenalin had done a number on her hormones, pumping her full of crazy endorphins that caused her body to jangle and sweat and crave like some kind of sex-starved junkie looking for a fix.

"So," he said, "what do you want?"

She needed to get herself back in the driver's seat and steer this show in *her* direction, show everyone who was boss. She sucked in a fortifying lungful of chilled night air.

"I…want…hot…chocolate."

So much for steering.

A few moments later, he handed her a steaming cup, the scent of chocolate curling through the air.

She tried not to stare as Adam puckered his lips to his cup. He must have gotten some kind of cue from Bradley, because suddenly he lowered his cup and looked up.

Cecily followed his gaze. For a moment, she thought they were staring at someone's home-made craft, a baseball decorated with leaves and little golden bows, suspended by a red ribbon from an evergreen branch.

And then she realized what it really was.

A mistletoe ball.

She looked back at Adam, whose blue eyes held a question. Feelings fluttered heatedly beneath her rib cage.

Oh, sure, she tried to remember all those things she'd been thinking mere seconds ago, but who the hell cared about who was in the driver's seat when there were so many other things to marvel at?

Like his scent, a mix of musky cologne and male. Or the hint of five o'clock shadow that shaded his jaw and climbed up over his lips.

Or, best of all, his mouth.

She'd noticed before that it was wide, full, beautifully shaped. But this time she also noticed its lived-in, been-around-the-block character. A mouth that was seasoned with experience. A mouth that undoubtedly hadn't been afraid to explore new tastes and textures. That had laughed, teased, welcomed strangers, customers, old friends. A mouth that wasn't uptight or forbidding, although it had weathered its storm of words and emotions. A mouth that smiled easily and grinned wickedly. That had surely stolen kisses when he was young, and ravaged and suckled in his prime.

She was tired of getting *this close* to that mouth and not having it. She wanted to taste it, share its wisdom, give back a little of her own.

Her heart thudding dully, she leaned closer.

Adam tilted his head, parted the lips of that amazing mouth. His eyes simmered with a need that made her body one big, hot, throbbing ache.

Steamy, forbidden spyware thoughts popped up in her brain. *Kiss me, take me, make me.* Contemptible as it was, she wanted the Stud Man and wanted him bad.

One of the crew emitted a low whistle. Bradley gasped.

The explosive currents racing through her slammed to a stop as a little voice inside her head asked, *Are you crazy? Sharing a first kiss in front of ten million people? Worse, a first kiss with your opponent that could cost you twenty-five big ones? Be alert!*

With an effort worthy of a superhero, she pulled back her puckered-up self.

"Sorry," she murmured.

He paused, releasing a pent-up breath. "No need to apologize."

When he reached forward, she closed her eyes, shuddering at the anticipation of his touch.

Something soft stroked her lips. Lightly, back and forth. Once. Twice. So soft, it was excruciating and exquisite all at once. The scent of roses engulfed her.

She opened her eyes.

Adam had pulled a rose from the bouquet and had touched one petaled bud lightly against her lips. A virtual kiss, sealing the moment without compromising themselves.

As though in a haze, she slowly re-entered the world. Became aware of the twinkling lights, the brisk air, a few sifting snowflakes.

The boom woman raised the pole holding the mike. A camera silently panned back. Sugar Megs crossed to Bradley, her footsteps crunching softly in the snow. Catching Cecily's eye, she held up her index finger.

One minute before the show ended.

One minute? Where had all the time gone?

Cecily straightened, darted a look for the teleprompter, when something familiar caught her eye.

The Well Suited jacket she'd made especially for tonight, blue with a touch of orange, lay on a chair just a few feet away. She could have sworn she saw Delores stash it in the costume trailer before the show, and yet there it was.

They were probably down to forty-five seconds now. Despite whatever heated interlude had just transpired between her and Adam, this was still a game and Cecily had to use the last seconds to her advantage.

But resurrecting a rule from her book felt too cold. No, instead she'd take advantage of a little free PR.

Had to be thirty seconds or less…

She made a beeline to the jacket, unbuttoning the orange monstrosity on the way. Bradley jumped to his feet and waved at a camera to follow her.

"Before the show ends," she said loudly, "I'd like to share one of my Well Suited—aagh." She hit a patch of ice and lost her balance, her arms flailing.

Strong arms caught her, scooped her into an embrace. Adam.

He leaned his head close to hers. "You okay?"

He held her so tightly, her body molded against his. Stray flicks of light played on his handsome face.

"I can walk," she whispered.

"Yes, but think of the ratings if you don't."

He swept her into his arms and carried her down a snow-shoveled path through a wonderland of glittering lights. Suddenly, a chorus of voices boomed behind them.

"Hallelujah!"

"And…cut!" yelled Bradley over a bullhorn.

"Cut!" yelled Sugar Megs.

"Cut," yelled a technician.

But Adam kept walking, holding Cecily in his embrace.

CHAPTER SEVEN

THE next morning, now officially called "De Morning-After Debriefing," as coined by Theodore, he and Cecily met for coffee at a different Starbucks. One she'd chosen because it opened into a bookstore and Cecily, who'd lost at *Marriage Material...or Misfortune?* last night, wanted to shop for something to help her regain her winning edge.

"Here's the deal, girlfriend," Theodore said between sips of his double-mocha-caramel-whatever as he and Cecily sauntered down an aisle between bookshelves. "If you'd made more love, not war, Adam wouldn't have won last night."

She frowned. "I didn't make war."

"Then why are you looking for that book?"

"Because Adam referred to *The Art of War*, and I want to know what he knows."

"Well, you two certainly weren't acting as though it was the art of war last night. That almost-kiss under the mistletoe…" Theodore dramatically clutched his chest. "Be still my beating heart."

Cecily felt her face go hot. "It was the moment."

"And a hell of a moment, too, may I add."

"How could I help myself? All those twinkling lights, the scents of spice and hot chocolate in the air, that big mistletoe ball suspended *right* over our heads." But it had been more than that. She'd wanted to taste Adam so bad, she hadn't even been able to think. Just feel and ache and want. She'd never had a moment like that with a man. *Never.*

Theodore leaned against a bookshelf and stared off into space. Because he carried a little extra weight, he loved to wear vertical stripes. Today he wore a pink and green striped shirt with French cuffs, designer jeans and oxfords. Cecily always viewed his style as the all-American gay boy. The latest men's fashion with two snaps for taste.

"And the way that hunky hunk of male scooped you into his arms and carried you off as the show ended…" With a dramatic sigh, Theodore fanned himself.

"Oh, my God," she suddenly said, "you voted for him, didn't you?"

Theodore stared at her in utter disbelief. "No way! As your almost-best friend, I'd never, ever betray you."

"You're hiding something."

"Okay. David voted for him."

"David?" She pondered the name for a moment. "We don't know any Davids."

"Yes, we do. The black-leather-jacket guy at Starbucks last week."

Her mouth dropped open. "You two are *dating*? Already? And you didn't tell me?"

"Yes, yes and, I think, yes. Reponses to questions phrased in the negative always confuse me. Anyway, darling, the point is you've been so stressed out with your TV series, the radio show, trying to rebuild Well Suited, I haven't wanted to wear you down with my love life."

"I want to be worn down!"

Theodore gently cupped her cheek with his hand. "Sweetpea, let's stay focused on you. Last night, Adam won the most votes because he broke his own rules. I think you should break your own rules, too."

"But—"

"But rules are made to be broken. That's what makes them fun to begin with. It's time for you to loosen up, dearest. Maybe not be so worried about what's perfect and be a little imperfect. Add some softness to your edginess and you'll have both men and women cheering you on *and* voting for you." He rubbed the sleeve of her jacket. "Corduroy?"

"Crushed velvet. You think I need to be softer, too?" She flashed on Delores's comment about the roses softening Cecily.

"Well, I think it would aid your cause to veer a bit from I Am Woman Hear Me Roar." He cocked his head, eyeing her jacket. "That rich turquoise color is divine. The splash of orange silk is a fabulous touch."

"I tried to wear it last night on the show but the director nixed it."

His mouth set in annoyance. "Enough's enough. We've got to stop these ghastly last-minute makeovers of you before airtime! They're stuffing you into jackets and coats that make you look like an antacid or a vegetable—"

"A pumpkin."

"Whatever. We need to find a way to show the world Cecily's fabulous urban-fem line of jackets."

"That's exactly what Megan said."

First thing this morning, Megan had called and had a heart-to-heart with Cecily about last night's voting results, where Cecily might have gone wrong, what she did right, how she needed more opportunity to promote her Well Suited jackets.

"She suggested I negotiate my wardrobe requirements with the producer."

Theodore snapped his fingers. "Instead of negotiating, let's demand."

She snorted. "I'm not some TV star prima donna."

"Darling, fake it." Looping his arm through hers, Theodore started walking her back down the aisle. "Instead of our scouring the shelves for *The Art of War,* let's go write a killer memo telling the producer your wardrobe requirements for the rest of the dates."

"Or I'll do what?"

"Walk. Who's he going to replace you with?"

"Any one of those PR-hungry, spandex-wrapped extras."

"No way. People want to see what's happening

between *you* and Adam, not some cookie-cutter blonde and Adam."

"I don't know."

They reached the door, which Theodore pushed open. "It's a dynamite idea. Trust me."

They stepped outside under the overcast skies of a chilly December day. "Like I've never heard a man say *that* before."

Five days later, on the eve of date number three, there was a knock at Cecily's apartment door at eight p.m.

She stuffed the last of a guacamole-laden chip into her mouth and stared at the door. Probably Theodore, anxious to know if she'd heard back from the producer after Cecily had faxed him her wardrobe requirements three days ago. She hadn't said she'd walk if her demands weren't met—which simply stated she wanted to wear her Well Suited jackets—but she had said the show could replace her if they didn't accept her terms. Not the way she typically did business, but Theo had said, "No guts, no glory," so she'd gone for it.

And considering a rival show had just today contacted Cecily, asking her to be a guest, she was betting *Marriage Material…or Misfortune?* would accept her wardrobe demand.

She glanced around her living room at the skimpy dresses and short skirts she'd hung up, trying to figure out what to wear tomorrow night. Oh, yeah, Theodore would get a kick out of this, seeing how Cecily was taking his advice.

She crossed to the door and peeked through the peephole.

Adam.

With a gasp, she pulled back. What was he doing here?

Knock, knock, knock.

She looked down at her red flannel underwear, her favorite winter jammies. She'd washed them so many times they were threadbare in a few key places. Hardly the kind of attire she wanted him to see her in.

Knock, knock, knock.

She leaned close to the door. "Adam," she said loudly, "isn't there a rule about our not fraternizing between dates?"

"I'm not fraternizing, just dropping by to wish you good luck tomorrow. And to assure you I won't be late again."

"Okay, thank you. Now you should go."

He lowered his voice. "Come on, Cecily, open up. It's weird talking through a door. I promise I won't come inside."

Yes, it was weird. Okay, she'd open it a crack and they'd wish each other good luck. Thirty-second conversation. What was the harm?

After sliding back the chain, twisting the deadbolt and clicking open the safety latch on the knob, she opened the door slightly and stuck her head around it.

"Hi."

He looked at her, a grin warming his face. "Hi. Sounds like you're opening Fort Knox."

"Yes, well. Safety and all that."

He wore a leather three-quarter jacket, which gave him a sexy, flashy look, over an open-necked sport shirt that showed a bit more chest than she'd been prepared for. She could see a few black chest hairs and imagined more running rampant over his chest before dwindling to a line that bisected his muscled diaphragm.

"Am I disturbing you?"

More than you know. "I'm, uh, getting ready for tomorrow," she whispered, feeling a spurt of jealousy that maybe he was dressed like that for someone else. "So, uh, you'll be on time for tomorrow's date?"

"Yes. I apologize for being late last time."

"You give great entrance."

"I know."

Something clicked in her mind. "You planned it that way, didn't you?"

"Yes," he said somewhat sheepishly. "But you should know, Bradley was in on it. He was prepared for you to start the show alone. He thought you'd rise to the challenge, and you did."

"Oh, great. I'm up against a good ol' boys' club."

"No." He shook his head. "I give you my word— no more double-dealing."

Cecily rolled her eyes. "Men."

Adam peered over her shoulder, his eyes lighting up. "And women," he said appreciatively, his voice turning husky.

She glanced over her shoulder, cringing when she

saw the leather skirt and bondage-leather halter top that poor Megan had been forced to wear on that date from hell. While clearing out her closet for potential hot-date outfits, Cecily had run across that and pulled it out thinking to donate it to Goodwill.

But there it was, in all its S and M glory for Adam to see.

When she looked back, Adam was fighting a smile. "Nice outfit."

"I was getting ready to toss it."

"Shame."

"Yeah, well, yesterday's styles and all that."

He cocked a questioning eyebrow.

"I mean…" A thought hit her. She didn't have to wait until tomorrow night to unnerve him, she could start right now. "Last season's dominatrix look is so passé compared to this year's, don't you think?"

Damn if the man didn't blush. "I—I wouldn't know."

"Oh, it is. Trust me. Thanks for dropping by."

And with that, she closed the door on a very confused man whom she'd be unnerving even more tomorrow night.

The next evening, six p.m. sharp, Cecily stood inside the Denver Art Museum entrance in her short black skirt, stiletto heels and her most sophisticated Well Suited jacket, which didn't have a whit of blue *or* orange. Because she'd been informed this date included an elegant dinner at a classy restaurant, she'd decided at the last minute to also wear a pair of dangling rhinestone earrings.

As Bradley approached he looked like a man either over-medicated or thoroughly miffed. Honest to God, she could see his mustache quivering from ten feet away.

"I read the producer's top-priority memo on your costuming requirements," he said, giving her a quick down, up look. "Guess we're not going for the European look," he sniffed.

She'd gotten word this afternoon that her memo had received the thumbs-up, which had given her ego a boost.

But rather than gloat her victory, Cecily thanked Bradley for getting the script to her two days in advance and listened attentively as he explained a few last-minute changes. When the show started, he explained, Adam would be seated at one of the tables within Palette's, the five-star restaurant inside the museum. Cecily would enter, cross to his table, and they'd pretend to order although both of their dishes would be premade.

"Adam had his grand entrance last week. You get yours tonight, Felicity; so make it big when you walk into the restaurant."

"Cecily. And I will."

She didn't comment about Bradley and Adam's scheming on the last date because the good ol' boys' club mentality wasn't, as she'd often told her listeners, something a woman should strain her brain cells over. She and Megan had even included a definition in their book's addendum, "Men A-Z", that took the air out of such testosterone tires:

> *The Good Ol' Boys' Club:* A sub-set of the male-dominated society, which is nothing more than a lame excuse for men to have all the fun.

As Bradley left Delores sidled up to Cecily.

"Excellent memo, dear."

"I didn't mean to usurp your position."

Delores chuckled a raspy smoker's laugh and shook her head. "I like your jackets. They show your character and creativity, and I say let's go for it."

"On the last date, did you leave my jacket on a chair where I could pick it up, promote my Well Suited line?"

"Now, would *I* go against Brad's edicts?" Delores's blue-gray eyes twinkled mischievously. "Back to tonight, I'm responsible for how you dress, so how's about showing me what you're wearing underneath the jacket."

"Before you react, hear my reasoning."

"React? This promises to be good."

Cecily unbuttoned her jacket and opened it slightly.

Delores arched a penciled-in eyebrow and gave Cecily a knowing look. "Going for the kill, are we?"

"I'm just trying the element of surprise, that's all."

"A surprise you're shielding from the camera, correct?"

"Absolutely."

Delores paused, thinking it over. "Bradley does have that five-second delay for any mishaps, but if you have a wardrobe malfunction it'll fall squarely on my shoulders."

"I won't get you into trouble, Delores, I promise. I'll be careful. It's just part of my ploy to take the lead away from Adam."

"Ploy to take the lead?" Delores chuckled again. "Still in denial about your feelings for him, I see."

"There's nothing to deny." Was there?

"Well, I'm pushing seventy. Soon, it'll be time for this girl to retire for good." Delores snapped a lighter to the end of a cigarette. The tobacco flared bright orange as she inhaled.

"Go get 'im, tiger," she said before walking away.

Adam sat at the table in Palette's, pretending to peruse the menu. Some of the extras were dressed as wait staff, their toned bodies wearing black chinos with white or pink designer dress shirts and ties. Classical music played softly in the background as extras sitting at nearby tables chatted and laughed softly.

"People, we're five…" Sugar Megs held up her hand, fingers splayed wide "…four…three…"

On one, she held up her index finger, then pointed it at Adam.

He smiled into the camera, reading the intro to this week's location.

"Welcome to Palette's, the elegant restaurant

located within the Denver Art Museum where tonight's date takes place. This evening, after we dine, we'll be visiting the American and European Art floor with paintings by Monet, Pissaro, Georgia O'Keeffe—"

The words stuck in his throat as he caught sight of Cecily making her entrance. Hoo-boy. He raked back his hair and exhaled a hefty breath. He couldn't believe his eyes. It was Cecily with legs. Long legs sheathed in shimmering black stockings that ended in a pair of black stilettos.

He swallowed, hard, thinking back to that dominatrix comment she'd made last night. He'd figured she was joking.

He was currently refiguring what he'd figured.

He watched her stroll toward him in long, liquid, panther-like strides. This woman, whom he'd tagged as a very cute and exciting but nevertheless rule-abiding retro-feminist, had suddenly morphed into a panther closing in on her canary boy.

Tweet tweet.

He stood, fumbled as he pulled out a chair.

She purred her thanks and sat down.

He sat, rubbing the flat of his hand over his jaw, his mind a muddle of thoughts, most of them over-heated. His mind, his body, this entire room was suddenly too damn hot. He grabbed the glass of water in front of him and drank. Draining its entire contents, he slammed the glass back on the table and sucked in a fortifying breath.

"Nice jacket," he croaked.

"Thank you. It's one of my Well Suited designs."

"Right. Urban—"

"Fem. For the woman who knows who she is. Let me show you the lining."

With her back to the camera, she opened the jacket and his brain dropped somewhere below his belt buckle as he stared at her sheer, skin-tight royal-blue top. No bra. Great tits.

This wasn't in *The Perfect Boyfriend.* Because he'd have damn well remembered it if it were.

"Like it?" she said sweetly, giving a little shimmy that caused a ripple effect that started at her shoulders and went all the way down to those nicely rounded, pink-tipped breasts.

White-hot heat shot through him like a laser. His mouth dropped open.

"Good." She rebuttoned her jacket.

He glanced at the teleprompter, realized he was supposed to be saying something about placing their order, but all he could muster was a primitive grunt reminiscent of his cavemen ancestors before burying his face into the menu.

After five or so minutes, during which time Cecily took the lead with the conversation, they were served their meals. A tropical fruit salad for Cecily, a French dip sandwich for Adam.

Cecily began eating, trying to act as though Adam weren't sitting there staring at her like a man who'd been stun-gunned. She'd wanted to throw him off by dressing in a short skirt, black leggings, stiletto heels, the pièce de résistance being "the flash" with, of course, her back to the cameras.

She figured women were howling with delight at her turning the tables while men relished her tactics. A sure way to woo back votes she'd lost on the last date.

What she hadn't counted on was Adam—the Stud Man, who claimed his con-fi-dence always would be rockin' and rollin' some babe's world—turning down-right Paleozoic. They'd received their scripts two days ago this time, but whatever lines Adam had memorized had devolved into a string of primal grunts.

She might feel sorry for him, but the guy had played a surprise role last date with his sensitive guy act. The very *last* thing she'd expected. Which was what she'd decided to give him this date—the very last thing *he* expected. What had he said to his bar regulars that day she'd walked in? That he was going to be one "misfortunate dude having to date that dominatrix librarian and her book of uptight rules"?

Well, say hello to the hottest librarian you've ever laid your baby blues on. Playing *femme fatale* wasn't a technique Cecily and Megan had advocated in their book, although, if a woman enjoyed the role, it certainly fell under their theory that *all* aspects of a woman's life were to be enjoyed and nurtured.

Which included sex.

She forked a piece of mango and bit into it, letting the fleshy fruit glide and slip against her tongue. She gave Adam a look that asked if he tasted as good.

He juggled his sandwich, nearly dropping it.

"Need help?" she asked.

He made a noise that sounded like "nugh".

Setting down the fork, she picked up a spear of pineapple with her fingers.

It took both hands, but he finally got a hold on his sandwich.

She held up the pineapple to better see it in the light, murmuring a throaty, "Nice."

He grunted.

Cecily lovingly flicked her tongue against the tip of the fruit, catching drops of the juice. Once, twice.

He dipped his sandwich into the au jus cup.

"Your fingers," she mouthed, waggling her free ones at the cup.

He did a double take at his digits submerged along with the sandwich in au jus and jerked the soggy sandwich out.

Something waved in her peripheral vision. She spared a glance over her shoulder at a frantic-looking Bradley, who was waving a sign that said in big black block letters, "Behave!"

She smiled sweetly, looked at Adam.

"Behave," she repeated, ignoring Bradley thumping his head with his fist. One of the crew chortled, then promptly shut up.

Adam gave her a look of astonished incredulity that said, *Me behave? You!*

"I can't wait to taste this," she whispered, her low and throaty tone causing the boom woman, her eyes wider than Adam's, to lower the mike so as not to miss any of the conversation.

Cecily leaned forward and slipped the fruit spear between her teeth and slowly sucked, making a throaty sound of appreciation at the rush of sweetness.

Adam made a sound like steam escaping.

She pushed the sweet, slick fruit further into her mouth, took a bite.

He bit off a hunk of sandwich, au jus juice running down his chin.

They chewed together for a long drawn-out moment, their faces flushed, their gazes locked.

More movement from the Bradley camp. Roger the production assistant had positioned himself where both Cecily and Adam could see him. From this vantage point, he was pointing with both hands at the teleprompter as though trying to land their attention back to the show. Simultaneously, Bradley was pacing the periphery of the set, waving another sign with the hastily scrawled message, "Can you two read?"

Cecily and Adam read the sign, glanced at each other, and started laughing like two kids caught passing notes in school. Suddenly it wasn't them against each other, but them against *them*. It felt good to let their guards down, to be on the same team and not pitted against each other.

"Shall we behave?" Cecily finally asked.

Adam set down his sandwich, cleared his throat. "I won't if you won't."

"Deal."

"And...cut!" barked Bradley over a bullhorn.

"Cut!" yelled Sugar Megs.

"Cu—"

"Shut up," snapped Bradley at the technician. "We've cut, already, okay?" He turned his attention back to Cecily and Adam. "Five minutes to get your behaving selves back together or I call the fire department."

CHAPTER EIGHT

"FELICITY," said Bradley, "you could have starred in *Tom Jones* with that eating scene, but please remember this is prime time, not cable, and children are watching."

Roger, wearing a Raiders baseball cap, shoved a diagram at Bradley, who scanned it and nodded his approval.

Bradley looked back at Cecily.

"I apologize for the *Tom Jones* moment," she said, knowing exactly the scene he was referring to because she'd watched a rerun of the movie last year with her grandmother. "Although, in all fairness, I wasn't *that* lascivious."

He gave her a look that said *Is that so?* "Although I have a five-second delay window, I'd prefer to not be frantically editing any future flashing incidents."

"It won't happen again."

"Is that a promise?"

"Yes."

With a weary sigh, Bradley turned his attention to Adam.

"And you," the director said, "losing the power to think or talk during an epicurean demonstration. Are you recovered enough to go live in—" he checked his Rolex "—four minutes?"

"Yes, Bradley," Adam answered. "It won't happen again."

"Is that a promise?"

Adam nodded.

"Well, I suppose we're safe considering no food is allowed in the art wing," he muttered, gesturing toward an archway that opened into the first exhibit. "We'll start with you two walking into the Renaissance Art display. Beyond that room are the Impressionist paintings, where camera two will pick you up. The teleprompter is always nearby, of course, and as you're aware the writers scripted some fascinating facts about some of the paintings."

He gave Cecily a look that said, *try to read it, will you?*

She nodded.

"Good. I have no doubt you two will find plenty of opportunities to sprinkle in ammunition from your books in the process. Ah, the course of true love."

As Bradley headed to his director's chair Delores stepped up to Adam. Her graying hair was pulled back in a ponytail, a pencil tucked behind her ear. She pulled a lint brush out of her pants pocket and began brushing his jacket.

"He's quite the cynic," he mumbled.

"He's been doing this show too long. Pressure's getting to him."

"If she flashes me again, I'm dead meat."

"She won't. She likes you."

"Hardly."

Delores tucked the brush back into her pocket. "You think she does fruit salad with just anyone? I don't think so."

He laughed. No, he didn't think Cecily did "fruit salad with just anyone", although she had seemed quite experienced with that pineapple spear.

The last thought was both arousing and vexing as he wondered if there was another man in her life. Did she have a boyfriend? He hadn't seen any signs of one when he'd peered into her living room last night, but that didn't mean one wasn't lurking around. Was the guy good to her? Was he supportive about her Well Suited business? Did he know that beneath the self-righteous, opinionated feminist exterior was a sensual, flashing woman?

Probably not. Because if this guy was all those things, she'd be, well, calmer. Happier. And even though he hadn't seen her sneaking a cigarette for a while, a decent boyfriend would be encouraging her to quit the nasty habit. Come to think of it, Adam should have written *The Perfect Boyfriend* instead of the perfect girlfriend book because as well as he knew men, he also knew women. And whomever Cecily was involved with, the bum wasn't worthy of her.

"You're clenching your fists," Delores murmured while adjusting the knot in Adam's tie.

"I hate the guy," he said tightly.

"Which one?"

"The one who has Cecily's heart."

Delores quirked a half smile. "Now, Adam," she said, as though talking to a child, "didn't your parents teach you to love yourself?"

Before he'd fully assimilated the meaning of the older woman's response, she was gone, walking briskly toward Bradley, who was managing a group of people hovering around his chair.

And Adam realized that for all the times he'd thought he had women pegged, the truth was they'd probably surprise him for the rest of his life. Delores with her Zen-like insights. And Cecily…

Was it possible he had her heart?

Damn if he didn't feel a rush of euphoria. Better than how he'd felt with his first crush, Suzanne Doyle, the smartest girl in his eighth grade class. Suzanne, his first love, first kiss, first broken heart.

All these years later, that crazy rush of first love washed over him again.

No, what he felt for Cecily wasn't love.

It was a shared sense of humor, a mind connection, a healthy dose of competitiveness, the urge to know her better, to take care of her, support her goals, bed her. Oh, yeah, especially that. To bed her, again and again, for the rest of their days.

But that meant kids. Family. A dog named

Humphrey or Sam or Prince. Several cats. School recitals. Paying for braces, piano lessons, college. God, how many kids were they talking?

"People, it's five!" yelled Sugar Megs, crashing through his reverie. She held up her hand, fingers spread wide.

I'm not in love.

"And four…three…two…one…"

She pointed at Adam and Cecily, and he had the jolting realization he was starting to know himself better.

Minutes later, he and Cecily strolled through the Renaissance Art section, its earth-red walls complementing the rich, vibrant colors in the detailed portraits and landscapes from the fourteen hundreds and fifteen hundreds. Cecily, true to her word to Bradley, kept her jacket buttoned and read diligently from the teleprompter. The director, standing next to the camera with his arms crossed, looked immensely relieved.

"This painting depicts Zeus," said Cecily, reading the scrolling words, "disguised as a satyr approaching the daughter of a river god with a sleeping Cupid signifying the union that is about to take place." Her eyes widened as she stared at the painting. "Wow."

Wow was right. He and Cecily stared in silence at the ripe-pink and very naked river-god daughter, who lay sprawled on a bed of fertile earth, staring up into the leering face of a robust and equally naked Zeus.

And Bradley had been worried about a fruit salad?

Cecily licked her lips. Adam shuffled his feet.

"The, uh, Renaissance painters were interested in the precise study of details," she continued, "and the entry of art into the real world of human experience."

She looked back at the painting. "Definitely detailed."

"Definitely the real world of human experience," he added drolly.

"Real. Right." She looked back at the teleprompter. "The paintings no longer sought to merely fulfill a function, but to challenge the person before it."

They stared at the painting again.

"I'm definitely challenged," said Adam, giving her a meaningful look.

"Shall we move on?" she croaked.

As they passed into the Impressionism exhibit, the walls changed from red to green. Bradley walked slowly along the perimeter of the set, like a grumpy schoolteacher ensuring his students were behaving. When he caught Adam's eye, the director signaled he'd like Adam to read the teleprompter next.

"Yes," Adam said, looking for the red light. He found the prompter, started speaking the lines.

"The Impressionist masters wanted to achieve a perfect reproduction of what the eye really perceived, so they believed that pictures should be created in the open air, in the very presence of what the artist was depicting."

He looked from the teleprompter to the painting he and Cecily stood in front of. "Whoa!"

It was a famous painting of a naked girl—well, except for wearing some baubles and heeled shoes—reclining on a bed. She looked directly at Adam, her dark eyes taking him in, and for a crazy moment he swore she looked like Cecily.

"Uh," he said, scanning the teleprompter for where he'd left off, "this painting is the infamous *Olympia*, which, when shown in eighteen sixty-five, aroused…" he swiped at the sweat forming on his forehead "…an unprecedented scandal. People believed the woman was a prostitute staring at the spectator while waiting for one of her clients."

He wished they were back at the botanical gardens surrounded by chilly night air because this museum was suddenly too stuffy, too hot, and if he was forced to talk about one more fleshy, naked painting, he'd go over the edge. This was no reality dating show; this was erotic hell.

"Is she waiting for a client?" Cecily cocked her head, checking out the picture. "I don't think so. Her hand's covering her…well, you know, which seems a demure gesture. Not one you'd expect from a hooker."

Bradley coughed loudly.

"Nice shoes, though," she quickly added.

Adam couldn't help but adore the look on Cecily's face. Flushed, a bit nervous, yet trying so damn hard to keep it together and be good after her fruit-salad theatrics.

Maybe instead of fighting this sexually surreal experience, he should try to enjoy it more. Relax. Not worry about the competition or getting votes or whether he was pissing off Bradley, but enjoy the time the way he might on a real date.

He slipped his arm through hers and pulled her closer to his side. He caught a whiff of her perfume, the scent deliciously familiar.

"To understand Manet," he said quietly, nodding to the painting, "is to appreciate he was an enigmatic, intriguing painter."

"What's enigmatic about a woman staring so boldly at us?" she whispered.

He lowered his head slightly, feeling Cecily's silky hair under his chin. "Maybe it's the question in her eyes."

The boom woman lowered her mike to catch their conversation, which had taken on an intimacy all its own.

"Contemporaries of Manet's were shocked by the brazen content of *Olympia*, but what they overlooked was the classic harmony of the composition. Check out the refinement of the whites and ivories." He shook his head in slow amazement. "It's one of the finest symphonies in white in the whole of art."

Keeping one arm looped through hers, he steered her to the next painting.

"And here," he continued, "*La Toilette* by Toulouse-Lautrec. You know, Lautrec liked to show women in the intimacy of their daily lives—dressing, doing their hair, washing themselves." As he spoke his fingers aimlessly caressed Cecily's arm. He heard her light intake of breath, the shudder of release.

"This is one of those rare works by Lautrec where the painter demonstrates no interest in the features of the model. He instead deliberately shows her from the back. Her torso is bare…" he slipped his hand to her back, gently grazing his fingertips along the textured fabric of her jacket "…and her red hair is caught in a chignon low on the nape of her neck."

His fingers moved up to her neck, and he slipped his hand underneath a spill of soft, curly hair. He stroked the soft, warm skin of her neck, feeling it prickle lightly under his touch.

Cecily wasn't sure where the sensual colors and the provocative images ended and her warm, drizzly, sexual feelings began. She was aware of Adam's fingers on her neck, the liquid sensation of skin on skin, a tingling that spread slowly, tickling her all over like stardust.

She felt as though it were someone else who'd barreled into this date hell-bent to win at all costs. Now she just hoped she didn't have a hormonal meltdown before Bradley yelled cut.

She realized neither she nor Adam had spoken for several long moments. Bradley was probably going apoplectic.

She glanced at the teleprompter, thinking to pick up wherever Adam had left off, but didn't recognize any of the words. Bradley's face loomed into her peripheral vision, giving her *that* look again. As if she were going to whip out a mango or something.

"I can't see where we are," she said under her breath.

"I wasn't reading the script." Adam shrugged. "Art is an old love of mine, especially Impressionism. After high school, I was torn between going to art school and studying painting or going to Duke and majoring in finance."

Art? Adam? This was like being informed The Hulk read Chaucer.

Although, she shouldn't be so surprised. The more she'd gotten to know Adam, the more she saw a sensitive side he'd been hiding under all that Stud Man posturing.

"So your parents insisted you study finance, right? My mom did the same thing. Threatened to not help me with my college tuition unless I studied business, although I was itching to study theatrical costuming."

"Well, only my dad insisted. My mother was behind my going to art school, so I did." A shadow passed over his face. "After a year, though, I switched to Duke and studied finance."

"Guess you finally saw your father's side."

"I'd seen it all along, but when he died, I wanted to fulfill his wishes."

She paused, feeling dreadful she'd probed. "I'm sorry."

"Don't be. It's what happens in life. We lose those we love." He looked around the room. "You know, other parents have a slew of photographs of their kids growing up, but mine had paintings. More portraits than I bet we see in this room. Pastels, oils, water colors, although my dad preferred oils."

A soft gasp escaped her. "Your father...was an artist?"

Adam nodded.

"And yet he didn't want you to go to art school?"

"If we'd had enough money, he'd have loved for me to formally study art. Dad was a talented painter, did everything from commissioned portraits to paintings for magazines, advertising agencies, et cetera, but sometimes the work was scarce. Twice we had to move because we couldn't make the rent, although my parents pretended it was for other reasons."

He glanced at the camera, raked a hand through his hair. "Whoa, didn't mean to spill all that on national TV."

She gazed up at Adam, feeling as though she were seeing him for the first time. So here was the real man. Not the one who boasted on the radio show, or ranted in his book, but *this* man. A man who held family dear, had an artistic side and yearned so deeply for what he'd lost that he'd rather keep running from emotional ties than allow himself to stop and feel.

"You?" he suddenly asked.

"What about me?"

He gestured to her jacket. "Who do you get your creative streak from?"

"My Grandmother Sims. My mom and I lived only a few blocks away, so I'd always be traipsing over to play her piano, help her in the garden. She's the one who taught me to sew."

"So we each have had a loved one who passed down a passion."

They stared into each other's eyes for a long, unguarded moment. Her gaze dropped to his mouth, that deliciously full, lived-in, been-around-the-block mouth. The room seemed to sway, the air tremble, and suddenly all she was aware of was his musky, masculine scent and the way his head cocked as he leaned closer...

The moment their lips touched, lightly and sweetly, it sealed something concrete within her heart.

"Cut," whispered Bradley, hovering nearby.

"Cut," echoed Sugar Megs.

"Cut," yelled the assistant director.

"Magnificent," Bradley said, marching across the set and throwing his arms around them. "You two were fantastic. Adam, you had our hearts when you talked about your father. Felicity, excellent improvised questions."

"Cecil—"

"And that kiss," Bradley cut in, emotion breaking his voice. "Perfect! Keep this up, and I'll be nominated for a Best Director Emmy."

Another Starbucks, another debriefing.

"Sweetpea," said Theodore, sipping his drink, "you were dynamite last night. And that *kiss*..." His voice trailed off and he gave her a you-she-devil-you look.

Everybody loved that kiss. Especially her. She'd obsessed on it all the way home after the show last night, all night long, all this morning. But that didn't change the fact she'd lost.

"Well, Adam was obviously more dynamite than me because he won."

"By only two votes!"

"But those two votes have probably cost me twenty-five thousand dollars."

"You have two more dates."

"If Adam wins again, that's it. No fifth date."

"Then we just have to make certain you win next time, darling, that's all."

"How?" She nibbled at her maple scone, which normally she loved but today tasted like cardboard. "I've been everything from the feminist to the *femme fatale* and it's done nothing for me."

A teenage girl with blue-streaked hair approached their table. She grinned, her teeth sparkling with braces. "Aren't you Cecily Cassell?" she asked, her voice rising. "The woman on *Marriage Material...or Misfortune?*"

Cecily looked surprised. "Yes."

The girl's lips trembled. "Is Adam a good kisser? My friend and I are dying to know."

"It, uh, happened rather quickly."

"Oh. Well, thanks." She scurried back to her pal. The two of them hunched together and giggled.

"Great," Cecily muttered. "I'm looking at the two votes that cost me my future."

He touched her hand. "I think your strategy for the next date should be simple, *very* toned down." He snapped his fingers. "I got it! Forget trying to be funnier or sexier or flashier—sorry for the pun—just be yourself on the next date. That'll *really* be the last thing Adam expects."

Her insides twisted. Had she been so eager to fight for the prize, to take on roles, that the man who had kissed her last night didn't really know the true Cecily?

"Sure," she said softly, although deep inside she was forming a game plan that had nothing to do with a gimmick or strategy or even being herself.

There simply wasn't going to be a next date.

Later that day, at five-thirty p.m., the regulars once again descended into Home Plate.

"Adam, my man," called out Rodney as he swaggered into the bar, "you do the men of the world proud!" He settled himself onto his favorite corner stool next to Larry, who was busily typing on a laptop. "What're you doin', college boy?"

"Writing a paper on the top ten fundamental cognitive principles of software design."

Rodney rolled a look at Adam. "We need to find a babe for this boy, and soon."

"Right," Adam said absently. "Soon."

He continued pouring beer from the tap, not really interested in the conversation, but then he'd not been interested in much today. He'd barely eaten breakfast, had done half his usual jog at Wash Park, had

had difficulty staying focused while preparing this month's accounts receivables.

He slid the glass of beer across the bar to Rodney as Tom, looking baleful as always, trudged into the place.

"Congratulations, Mr MacGruder," he said, his baritone voice booming through the bar area. "You were a gentleman last night despite the woman's questionable food tactics. MacGruder's Marauders is one game away from being a done deal."

Rodney snorted. "Speaking of questionable tactics, what'd she look like under that jacket, Stud Man? The real things or fakes?"

"You guys are gross." Adam grabbed a highball glass.

"Greetings, gentleman!" said Vince loudly as he strolled into the bar like a gladiator after a win. "Say hello to Vince Barbieri, vice president."

"Congrats, Vince!"

"Way to go!"

Adam smiled. "I knew you'd get the promotion. Let me buy you a drink."

"Thank you, and make it my usual. I might be a big shot executive, but I'm still a beer-drinking guy at heart." He flipped his striped silk tie over his shoulder as he sat down. "Everybody looked pretty dour when I first walked in. What'd I interrupt?"

"Adam was avoiding the question posed to him by Rodney," answered Tom as he carefully folded his coat over the stool next to him.

"Which was?" asked Vince.

"Rodney wanted to know what Adam saw when the dominatrix librarian flashed him," said Larry, typing.

"Look, I called her that before meeting her," said Adam, sticking a lime into the mouth of a beer bottle and handing it to Vince.

"So, buddy o' mine," Vince said, squeezing the lime, "what *did* you see?"

Adam grabbed a bar towel and dried a glass. "You guys need a life."

"Stud Man, 'fess up," Rodney chortled.

"That's right," chimed in Larry, looking up from his computer. "Did you stay up all night doing the horizontal Watusi?"

"I call it the vertical rumba," offered Vince.

"I'd settle for a slow waltz," muttered Tom.

"That's enough!" Adam tossed the bar towel onto the bar and glared at them.

The guys froze, all staring at him. The only sounds were the click of pool balls and the muted chatter of CNN from the far room.

"Don't you ever want to talk about sports or the weather or even what's happening in the Middle East? Why does the conversation have to be about ol' Adam and whether he scored last night? Do I probe your dating lives?"

"We don't have any," murmured Larry.

"Speak for yourself," said Vince, who, after glancing over his shoulder at the front door, suddenly turned serious. "You have a guest, Adam."

Heads turned.

There stood Cecily, a dubious expression on her face, her hands shoved in the pockets of an oversize red fleece jacket.

"Sorry to interrupt," she finally said.

The guys grunted unintelligible responses and became preoccupied with their drinks.

Adam felt the weight of irritability he'd been carrying all day suddenly lift. "Want to sit over there?" He gestured toward the table in the corner where they'd sat the other time she'd dropped by unexpectedly.

A few moments later, he lowered himself into the chair opposite Cecily. She wore a pink turtleneck that matched the flush of her cheeks. She'd draped her fleece jacket on the back of an extra chair.

"Doesn't look like one of your Well Suited designs."

She barely smiled. "Don't have one for cold weather, so I tossed on a jacket an ex left at my place."

"Ex," he repeated. "So…that means you're not currently involved with anyone?"

Her eyebrows shot up in surprise. "I wouldn't have agreed to do the show if there'd been a significant other."

"Me neither."

"Bull."

"Okay, so I was dating several women, but that stopped after the show started."

She flashed him an incredulous look.

"Meaning…" he shifted in his seat "…I'm only dating you."

"But, it's not reality, dating in front of millions of viewers, even if they call it reality TV."

"Well…" He placed his hand on hers. "Maybe it could be."

She went very still, her eyes studying his. "I came here to tell you I can't do this anymore."

"This?"

"These shows. I can't play games, can't pretend I'm someone I'm not." She took a deep breath. "I'm quitting, Adam."

CHAPTER NINE

TEN minutes later, the front door to Home Plate closed behind Cecily with a loud click.

Adam, still sitting at the table where they'd been talking, looked out the window and watched her walk down the snow-shoveled sidewalk toward the Sixteenth Street Mall shuttle. Had he ever before noticed that bounce to her walk? *Too much energy in one body.* She'd mentioned once that she devoured mysteries, but it was difficult to imagine her sitting still long enough to read a book.

Even more difficult to digest what she'd just said.

Blowing out a gust of breath, Adam rose and headed to the bar. He surveyed everyone's drinks, mostly to avoid their group stare.

"Larry, another Arnold Palmer?"

"Sure, thanks."

Tom cleared his throat. "Adam, we apologize for being offensive earlier."

Rodney made a disgruntled sound. "Hey, we were just being ourselves. Since when is that offensive?"

Somebody shushed him.

Adam scooped ice into a glass, the clattering sound of the cubes almost deafening in the sudden quiet. He knew what they were waiting for.

"She wants to quit the show," he finally said.

Vince did a double take. "No way!"

"Why?" asked Larry.

Adam poured lemonade into the glass. "Said she's tired of pretending she's someone she's not."

"Well, if she's not who she's been, who the hell is she?" asked Rodney.

Somebody shushed him.

Despite his somber mood, Adam smiled. "Remember that tag line for her line of jackets? 'For the woman who knows who she is'? Well, I think that describes Cecily Cassell."

"And to think I was already tellin' the guys at work about MacGruder's Marauders," mumbled Rodney.

"According to my calculations," Larry said, looking up from his computer, "you had a fifty-five-percent chance of winning the next date."

Tom shook his head. "You guys are in mourning and no one's died. She won't quit because, if she tries to, she'll be slammed with lawsuits from advertisers, the television station, her radio show and others who are counting on making money off the show. Shame if she insists, though, because I read the contract and Adam or Cecily must win the most votes for *three* dates out of five to win the prize money. Adam's won *two*. If for some reason she walks, he wouldn't win by default."

"Did you remind her of that clause?" asked Vince.

"No." Adam crossed to the sink, began washing a few glasses. "I quoted Vince Lombardi and told her once you learn to quit, it becomes a habit."

He'd always liked that quote. Believed it, too, but the truth was he'd repeated it to Cecily because he couldn't stand the thought of her quitting *him*. When he'd suggested they could date for real, she hadn't answered. Which in Adam's book said more than a simple "no".

It was tough to admit to himself that he'd misread her. That all this time he'd thought they were nursing crushes on each other, it'd been one-sided.

"She'll stay," said Vince matter-of-factly. "It's easier to go through one or two more dates than wrestle with lawsuits forever."

"If my fifty-five-percent calculation is correct," said Larry, "we're only a week away from being a team!"

Several of the guys cheered.

Adam straightened and surveyed the group as he dried a glass. They were a mixed bag—college egghead, lawyer, hardware store employee, vice president. Add the others who'd asked to be signed up with MacGruder's Marauders and they had quite a pack.

"We'd cream the competition," said Vince. "Remember our team at Duke?"

Adam smiled. "Yeah. Good times." He, Vince and a bunch of loose-ends had formed a rag-tag soccer team their sophomore year at college and entered the city competitions on a lark. Damn if they hadn't won the title two years running. And laid more soccer groupies than he'd thought possible. Having just lost his dad, Adam had valued the friendships more than ever.

"I agree, she'll most likely stay," said Tom. "Which means she'll play tougher than ever because she'll need to win to stay in the game. If I were you, Adam, I wouldn't let your guard down for a millisecond."

"Remember that saying from *The Art of War*," said Vince, "'All warfare is based on deception.'"

"Let's hear it for Sun Tzu!" said Tom, hoisting his bottle.

"Here, here!" said Larry.

"Adam, you with us?" asked Rodney.

It was a rallying of the boys again. And, to be honest with himself, it felt good to be back. Maybe he'd taken this whole dating three-ring-circus too seriously, convincing himself he felt something deeper for Cecily when all they'd been doing was playing the dating game. As he often counseled men in his chapter "The Seven Highly Effective Techniques of the Seducer", it was critical to know when to fold 'em, when to hold 'em.

Adam needed to fold 'em. It was time to get his head on straight and walk away from romance.

He lifted a glass of water. "To MacGruder's Marauders."

Standing behind the sole cameraman and his handheld camera, plus the boom woman who operated a compact mike, Bradley listened attentively to the studio techs on his cell phone. Because of the crowded conditions of this location, he was working with a skeleton tech crew—no room for Wardrobe, Make-up, production assistants, lighting techs, hangers-on. Bradley had already told Adam if something ripped, or a cowlick popped up, tough.

Bradley held up five fingers.

The countdown for date number four was starting and Adam wished he were anywhere but here.

Four fingers…

Cecily was a no-show.

Three…

He'd lost twenty-five thousand dollars.

Two.

He'd never get suckered into something like this again. *Ever.*

Bradley held up his index finger, then pointed to Adam.

"Greetings and welcome to date number four," he said, raising his voice to compete with the hockey fans screaming in the arena seats around him. "We're coming to you live from an Avalanche hockey game against the Minnesota Timberwolves at the Pepsi Center in the mile-high city of Denver."

On the rink, a fight broke out. The crowd surged to their feet and roared.

When the sound subsided, Adam continued. "The Pepsi Center seats eighteen thousand, has ninety-five luxury suites, a sixty-thousand-pound score-board center court, six locker rooms and one guy on a date for two because Cecily Cassell, it appears, decided to quit."

Bradley gave Adam a pitying look, and Adam accepted it. Hell, he had the right considering twenty-five thousand big ones had floated out of his life into nowhere land.

"So," he continued, "while we have these last few minutes together, let me thank you for tuning in. If you're ever in Denver, drop by my sports bar, Home Plate, and I'll treat you to a brewski. Just don't all ten million of you show up at once, okay?" He forced a laugh.

"Our director, Mr Bradley F. Crown, has asked me to inform you in lieu of tonight's regular programming, the network movie of the week will be starting an hour early, so stay tuned."

Bradley, listening to someone on the other end of the cell phone, made a rolling "keep talking" motion.

"Did I mention the scoreboard hanging at center court weighs sixty thousand pounds?"

Bradley nodded and held up two fingers, meaning it was the second time Adam had mentioned it.

"Okay, let me bring everyone up to date on tonight's score. Avalanche zero, Timberwolves zero, Adam two to one."

The crowd whooped and screamed as the Avs center blasted the puck past several Timberwolves to an Avs teammate.

Bradley held up a piece of paper on which he scrawled the number twenty-five.

Adam frowned. Oh, he got it. "Uh, some of you might be wondering what I'll be doing with that twenty-five-thousand-dollar prize. The answer is… nothing. Nada. Zilch. Unfortunately, it's in our contracts that if either of us drops out before one wins three dates out of five, the other doesn't win by default. Terms of the deal. A real shame."

"I know," said a familiar voice.

He looked up.

Cecily stood in the aisle, wearing a pair of snug black corduroy pants, a hip-length plush turquoise jacket over a white blouse, and flats. The colors set off her dark hair and pink skin and, God, she looked more beautiful every time he saw her.

Bradley, frantically talking into his cell, motioned to the cameraman to cover Cecily.

She chewed on her bottom lip. "Sorry I'm late. I got a new driver, and he lost my address."

"Uh, no problem." Adam stood, indicating for her to take the seat next to him.

She sat down and looked at him with big dewy eyes. "I couldn't let you down," she whispered.

He smelled her cologne, the scent going straight to his brain. When she realized they were staring at each other as though the eighteen thousand people around them didn't exist, she flushed slightly and lowered her gaze. She looked so guileless, so sweet.

He didn't believe it for a moment.

She was up to something. This was the surprise

tactic Tom had warned him to watch for. Last date she'd come on like ball busters, doing an erotic eating scene that could've put her in the Fruit Bowl Hall of Fame. And this week she was suddenly Rebecca of Sunnybrook Farm?

"Thanks for not letting me down," Adam said. *You had to come or they'd have sued your ass.*

Oh, yeah, he had her number. It was time for him to play the game again as the Stud Man, be on the watch for her moves, not underestimate her tactics.

"I've never been wild about live sports events," Cecily said, "especially hockey."

The crowd surged to its feet as another fight broke out on the ice. The fans screamed and booed, some punching the air with virtual hits.

"Gee," Adam said loudly, "why not?"

She caught his sarcasm and gave him a withering look. "Because everybody's so laid-back." She shivered, wrapped her arms around herself.

"You're not cold, are you?"

"It's more mental than physical, I know, but I wish I'd worn a warmer jacket."

"I don't have a coat to offer you, but want my sweater?"

Her gaze slid down and up. He felt a shock of sheer lust that threatened to undermine his determination.

"What are you wearing underneath your sweater?"

"Nothing." He waggled his eyebrows.

She smirked. "I think there's a dress code here. No shoes, no shirt, no game."

He shrugged. "Okay, just wanted to help."

The crowd screamed again. A guy with a face painted red and white, the Avs colors, leaned over them and shouted, "Sakic, don't be a nancy!"

After the frenzy subsided again, Adam leaned toward Cecily. "Hungry?"

"A little," she murmured, her smile almost as intimate as a kiss.

Oh, she was good. Really, really good with this good-girl, bad-girl act.

He fished a twenty out of his pocket. "Get whatever you want, baby. I'll take a brat and beer."

He was taking his own advice from *The Perfect Girlfriend*'s list of "Things to Do to Keep Her on Her Toes":

Number four. When at a sports event that she doesn't really care for anyway, let *her* do the snack-bar runs. Hey, you've lived your entire life to catch the next touchdown, slam dunk, goal— you want to miss it, dude? But just to show you're not a total bum, tell her to keep the change.

"And keep the change."

She mouthed something, the words absorbed in a torrent of catcalls and boos from the spectators at something that had just happened on the ice.

"No problem," he said, wondering if she'd always had the vocabulary of a sailor, "I'll get it. What would you like?"

She visibly brightened. "Do they have margaritas

and tacos? Ooh, a chicken taco with a little guaca-mole would be fantastic."

He looked around, spied a kid carting a tray. He waved the bill to get his attention.

"Two beers, two brats!" Adam yelled.

A few minutes later, Cecily watched Adam stuffing his face with a hot dog and wondered when he'd regressed into the Stud Man. And to think she'd decided to stay in the game because it wasn't fair to quit. Although to be absolutely truthful with herself, she'd known she'd miss Adam. This past week, she'd thought a lot about their last date, their shared experiences and that too-brief kiss at the end.

And even more, she'd thought about Adam's comment, suggesting their dating might go beyond this show. At the time, she'd been too taken aback to respond, but since then she'd thought how they seemed destined for more.

So the last thing she'd expected was to show up tonight and be confronted with the old Adam, the full-of-himself, con-fi-dent male. Was he miffed because she was late? Not his style to overreact like this. Her feminine intuition said he was once again pushing the rules from his book, going for the big play because if he won tonight's date, he won the twenty-five grand.

Well, two could play at this game. *I'm not out of the running yet, Stud Boy.*

"How's your hot dog?" Adam asked around a mouthful of food.

"Tastes just like a taco."

A beefy guy staggering up the stairs stopped next to them.

"Hey," he bellowed, pointing, "it's the perfect couple!" He looked back at a red-haired woman following him. "Honey, it's those perfect people you like."

Another woman in the row in front of them turned to look. "Oh, my gawd," she squealed, "it's them!"

A camera flashed in Cecily's face. She blinked, seeing splotches of dancing yellow in front of her eyes.

"Hey, sweetheart," someone said, "you're dripping mustard on your jacket."

Cecily looked down and spied a big glob of yellow running down her turquoise Well Suited jacket. Tonight was proving to be one big mess. She'd been late. Adam had reverted to a Cro-Mag. She'd messed up her jacket, which messed up her advertising opportunity, which messed up the rest of her life, although possibly it wasn't that bad yet and she was merely being hysterical.

At least nothing worse could happen.

"Woo hoo, great kiss last week, dude man!" A forty-something male wearing a red Avs sweatshirt that barely covered his paunch and a pair of felt moose ears stuck on his head gave a thumbs-up to Adam. When Adam flashed him back a thumbs-up, moosehead emitted another, "Woo hoo!" and started doing some kind of gyrating dance.

Something like an alternate universe caught her eye. She swerved her gaze, a cold horror filling her as she stared at the screen on the giant scoreboard center court. It flashed an image of a dancing, moose-headed man for the entire arena to see. In the lower-left corner was a wide-eyed woman, her mouth open, an unmistakable glob of yellow on her turquoise jacket.

What idiot said there was no such thing as bad PR?

"And…cut," said Bradley.

"Okay, we're off the air," he said into his cell. "I'll explain the plan to them, call you back in a few."

He punched a button and dropped the phone into his shirt pocket. "Who the hell had the bright idea for date number four to be at a hockey game?" he said with a heavy sigh.

The cameraman and the boom woman looked at each other and shrugged.

Bradley leaned closer to Cecily and Adam and lowered his voice.

"This isn't going to work. Inebriated fans are recognizing the two of you and it's only going to get worse. Unfortunately, we're not set up to quickly move to another location. So here's the deal."

"Woo hoo!"

Bradley visibly flinched. "Hockey fans," he muttered under his breath before continuing. "In exactly three minutes, you two will get up and leave. The camera and boom will follow you upstairs, through the snack-bar area and out the exit to a limo waiting in the parking lot."

"Woo hoo hoo!"

Bradley paused. "Please improvise, which I *know*

you two can do, as we'll continue broadcasting live until you get into the limo." He looked at Adam. "By the way, the camera loves you. If you're ever interested in an acting career, look me up."

Adam swallowed the last bite of hot dog. "Thanks, Bradley."

The director shifted his gaze. "And, Felicity—"

"Cecil—"

"Can you get that mustard off your jacket as soon as possible?"

"Woo hoo," she said with a forced smile.

Three minutes later, Cecily and Adam were walking up the stairs to the snack-bar area followed by the cameraman, boom woman, Mr Woo Hoo and several drunken people who were more enthralled with following reality-TV stars than watching hockey.

They reached the top of the stairs and began weaving their way through the crowds in the concession area. Fryers crackled, scents of hamburger and fries hung in the air, vendors hawked Avalanche posters and T-shirts.

And more people were recognizing them.

"Stud Man!"

"Hey, Cecily!"

"Great kiss last week!"

Adam darted a glance at her. She pretended not to notice even though every cell of her body was tingling being near his presence. Like it or not, her feelings for him had intensified these last few weeks. Her body's need to experience him, too. All of him.

She'd been so sure the feelings were reciprocal. Yet tonight Adam was acting as though they'd barely met. She wished she could dismiss it easily, or at least *pretend* to, but she couldn't. Somewhere along the way, she'd done what she hadn't been prepared to do again for a long time. She'd opened her heart to love and she wasn't sure if that pissed her off or pleased her.

"Hey, kiss again!" called out some guy.

"Dream on," Cecily muttered, grabbing a napkin off a condiment stand they were walking by.

"I heard that," said Adam.

"Good." She paused, dabbing at the glob of mustard on her jacket, glad to have a distraction.

"Was I that bad a kisser?"

"It was awfully quick," she murmured, shooting him a look. Damn, the man was good-looking. "Difficult to tell."

"It wasn't *that* quick."

She smiled impishly. "Barely a lip touch, as I recall."

"Well, hard to build up steam when everybody's yelling 'cut'—"

"Hey, could you autograph this for my aunt?" A rotund guy sporting a beard shoved a piece of paper that looked suspiciously like a hamburger wrapper at Adam. "Write To Bob."

Adam did a double take at the guy, then started writing. "Plus," he muttered under his breath for Cecily's ears, "we were being watched by millions of people. Not exactly an encouraging ambience for lip-locking."

"And what might such an encouraging ambience be?" she whispered.

He gave her a look that said if she used that suggestive tone again, anywhere in the damn world would do.

"Cecily, your autograph, please!" A teenage boy thrust a plastic CD case at her.

"You want me to sign a CD case?"

The kid nodded. "Make it out to your perfect boyfriend Mike."

More people appeared, calling their names, waving paper and other paraphernalia for them to sign. The cameraman and boom woman jockeyed to keep their places. Somebody spilled part of a beer on Adam's sweater.

He brushed at it, assuring the man it was no problem, then shot a look at Cecily. She raised her eyebrows. And at that moment, as though connected by a telepathic link, she knew exactly what he was thinking.

He darted a glance at the Exit sign on the far wall, looked back at her.

She nodded.

He grabbed her hand. "Let's go!"

As they started running toward the exit, Cecily gave a small prayer of thanks she'd thought to wear flats tonight.

Adam glanced over his shoulder. "Cameraman's still with us!"

She glanced in the reflection of a window they were running past. Sure enough, the cameraman and boom woman were running behind them, with several people following in their wake.

Cecily started laughing, imagining what people at home were watching. Adam and Cecily's heads bobbing, the huffing and puffing of the boom woman with the mike, a faint "woo hoo" in the background.

They hit the exit door, ran outside into the chilly night air, and halted, their heaving breaths escaping in plumes of white. Cecily grinned, loving Adam's full-lipped smile.

The competitors were once again a team.

Adam looked around. "Where's the limo?"

All they saw was a parking lot full of vehicles.

"I think we headed out the wrong exit," murmured Cecily.

The cameraman and boom woman burst through the door, staggering to a stop as they pointed their instruments at Adam and Cecily.

Just then, a taxi eased to a stop near the curb, its dome light on.

"Looks like a limo to me," Adam yelled, grabbing Cecily's hand.

They jogged to the taxi and jumped into the back seat. The inside was blissfully warm. Beads hung on the rearview mirror. An old Led Zepplin tune played on the radio. The taxi driver, a fifty-something guy with a long ponytail, looked over his shoulder at them. "Where to?"

A light flooded the inside of the taxi.

"Wow," said the taxi driver, peering at it.

"It's a camera," explained Adam, locking his door. Cecily did the same. "We're live."

"Better than the alternative, man." The taxi driver blinked into the light as several people started pounding on the windows.

"I love Adam!" yelled a hefty woman with freckles.

"Wow," said the driver again, checking out the growing number of people crowding around the cab.

"I think we'd better go, like *now*," said Cecily.

"Cool." The driver stepped on the gas, honking the horn. People finally stepped back and they drove away.

"You people rock stars or something?"

"We're on a TV reality dating show," answered Adam. "*Marriage Material...or Misfortune?*"

The taxi driver shrugged. "Sorry, don't watch TV. Where to?"

Adam edged closer to Cecily. An eyebrow shot up. "We started off the evening rather badly," he murmured huskily, touching a curl of her hair. "How about we end it on a better note?"

He gave the curl a gentle tug, pulling her toward him. Her mouth was an inch away from his, and she could feel his warm breath on her lips.

"Come home with me," he whispered.

CHAPTER TEN

THE taxi driver, while waiting to hear the answer to, "Where to?", eased out of the Pepsi Center parking lot and headed slowly down Speer Boulevard toward downtown Denver with its columned skyline and blue Qwest sign. From the backseat, Adam checked the road ahead. In another block, he'd need to tell the driver whether to continue heading south or take the turn north.

"I'm not a mind reader," Adam whispered, cupping Cecily's cheek with his large, warm hand. "You don't answer, I'll guess wrong. Been there, done that."

"You did?"

"When I suggested we could date outside of the show…" His voice trailed off.

"Oh." Had he been nursing a wounded-male ego for the past week because she hadn't responded to his comment when she'd dropped by Home Plate? Was that part of his Neanderthal regression tonight? Yep, she definitely had a sensitive man on her hands.

"Your comment came just as I was telling you I was quitting," she explained. "Rather than get sidetracked, I just barreled ahead with my announcement."

He shook his head, chuckling. "I should've known. You're definitely a single-minded woman."

Woman? Appeared Adam MacGruder was not only sensitive, but more enlightened than he let on.

She pulled away slightly and watched how the passing street lights flickered shadows and light on his face. He was one of those men who had a naturally rough, sexual look. Yet tonight she saw more. A subtle despondency, or maybe a loneliness, that needed the balance of softness.

"Yes," she whispered, "take me to your home."

His face relaxed into a smile. He gave his address to the driver, then leaned back against the seat and tugged her closer.

"You keep me on edge, Cecily. Never had a woman turn my world every which way but loose before."

"Could say the same about you, too," she teased, nestling against him, liking the feel of his stubbled cheek against hers. She eased in a long breath, taking in his scent, welcoming its familiarity.

With the gentlest pressure of his thumb, he angled her head.

"The other kiss was too short, too quick," he said, his voice dropping to a husky tone. "Let's fix that."

He studied her for a moment and her stomach clenched in anticipation. When he closed the space between their lips, she felt her breath flee her body.

Replaced by his.

At first, their lips merely touched. Softly, tentatively. *This* was their first kiss, just for the two of them, and she willed herself to always remember this moment, remember how soft yet firm his mouth was on hers, the way his tongue lightly, invitingly touched her lip, the heat of his ragged breath on her skin.

Remember, remember.

A deep, hungry sound rumbled in his throat as he kissed her more firmly. She opened her mouth, inviting him, and he slid his tongue inside, tasting her in slow, broad strokes.

The taxi soared down streets, eased between lanes as the radio played a throbbing, pulsing tune. Her head spun, her heart pounded as she lost herself in the sweet, wicked heat of their kiss.

Adam suddenly pulled back, nudged her head aside with his, and buried his face into the crook of her neck.

"You smell so good," he murmured.

She shuddered a sigh as he planted burning kisses on her neck, up to the sensitive patch of skin behind her ear, along her jaw, until he reached her lips again and devoured them with a long, soulful kiss she felt all the way down to her toes.

Liquid heat, like hot silken ribbons, spilled into every secret part of her body, rippling through her breasts, her stomach, down her thighs, leaving her body perched on a precipice, aching for more, more...

"Adam, oh Adam," she murmured, arching her body against his, groaning as their tongues tangled, danced, retreated, teased. She moved convulsively against him, felt his hardness pressed against her thigh, the light teasing trail of his fingers around her breast. Not enough, needed more.

Tearing her lips from his, she struggled for breath, her chest heaving. For a single, suspended moment, their gazes locked and they stared deeply into each other's eyes.

"You're good," she whispered hoarsely.

"You're better."

She grinned, dove back for more.

Needs exploded through Adam as he devoured her warm, ripe mouth, tasted her sweet, hot flavors with his tongue. He made love to that mouth, sliding, lapping, flicking his tongue in and out with increasing tempo.

On the radio, the Stones sang urgently about spending the night together. Outside the window, snowflakes whirled dizzily in the churning winds. The world coalesced into sensations of skin, heat, taste…

Time ceased to have meaning. He could spend the rest of his life kissing her, over and over.

Suddenly, he was aware the taxi had stopped. Grudgingly, he separated from the kiss and stared blearily at the gray outside the window.

"Denver never gets fog," he rasped.

"No, you steamed up the windows," said the driver.

Adam rubbed a circle with his hand on the glass, clearing a view. Sure enough, there was his building.

As Cecily adjusted her clothing Adam pawed in his pockets for his wallet. After paying the driver, they stumbled out of the cab, the blast of chill tempering their overheated bodies.

As the driver drove off he flashed a peace sign out his window.

Except for taking the elevator to the tenth floor, Adam was fairly certain he and Cecily ran all the way to his apartment.

As they kissed outside the door Adam fumbled in his pockets for his keys, finally ripping away from a kiss long enough to find the right one, then groping and scrabbling and swearing until—on the third try—he shoved the damn thing into the lock.

Click.

They fell inside. He slammed the door shut with his foot while flicking the light switch. A single ceiling lamp pooled light into the entranceway.

"Would you…like a…drink?" he asked between ragged breaths.

"Hell, no," she whispered, peeling off her jacket and tossing it aside.

"Me neither," he choked before moving his mouth over hers. The next thing he knew, he had her pressed up against the wall, his mouth ravaging hers, his senses on overload, his body bombarded with a carnal need so fierce, it was a miracle he hadn't imploded by now.

He broke the kiss and looked into her slitted eyes. "Are we going…too fast?"

Her blouse was partially unbuttoned, exposing the

top of a full breast spilling out of a pink lacy bra. White-hot heat shot straight to his groin.

He forced his gaze back to hers.

"Too fast?" she repeated incredulously, panting. "Hell, no."

Buttons popped as she ripped off her blouse, followed by her bra. Trying to watch her while tugging off his sweater, he got his elbow wedged in a wayward sleeve. Momentarily, his head was stuck inside his sweater as Cecily, in a series of frantic movements, managed to dislodge his elbow and drag the article of clothing over his head.

She hurled it aside.

They both suddenly froze as they took in each other's naked torsos.

"You're better than Michelangelo's *David,*" Cecily murmured,

She'd seen naked men before, but none of them had looked *this* good. The ceiling light poured a pale amber glow, like butter, over his muscled form. The chestnut hair that sprinkled his corded forearms also carpeted his chest, narrowing to a thin line that snaked down his rippled abdomen before disappearing into the waistband of his slacks.

In which she saw a noticeable bulge.

"Yummy," she whispered, reaching for his belt buckle.

He stepped forward and caught her hands, lifting them over her head and pressing them against the wall.

"Hold on," he murmured huskily, "I'm not through."

She felt the heat of his gaze as it traveled over her. He imprisoned her wrists with one hand, letting the other stroke and knead her mounds.

"So beautiful," he murmured, drawing lazy circles around one nipple, then the other, his touch light, teasing, tormenting….

Taking in a shaky breath, she arched her back slightly, thrusting out her suddenly full and overwhelmingly achy breasts.

"Oh, yes," he growled, releasing his hold on her while he lowered his head. He touched the tip of his tongue to a nub, flicking it once, twice, teasing, playing, tormenting her.

Hot and needy, Cecily grabbed his head with both hands and held it to her breast, rubbing an erect nipple back and forth across his mouth. "Take me," she whispered urgently.

With a conspiratorial groan, he drew it into his warm, moist mouth and suckled.

She bit her lip, the magic of his mouth causing her internal temperature to spiral even higher. While he moved to the other breast and sucked and licked and nipped a tightening worked its way down between her legs, engorging her with need.

She reached for his belt buckle again.

Damn if the man didn't step back.

"First, I need to get something," he murmured huskily.

He disappeared into the dark, leaving her alone,

half naked, and panting. She heard the muffled noises of a cabinet opening and closing, then his returning footsteps.

She toed off her shoes, kicked off her pants and was damn near jogging in place by the time he returned.

Somewhere between here and there, he'd shed his pants, too.

They paused again, stared at each other's bodies.

"Yummy," he said, grinning.

She smiled, liking their play of words. Plus, the way he looked at her gave her an incredible rush of feminine power. It was exhilarating and exciting to feel beautiful and desired, a feeling she hadn't experienced in way too long.

His gaze traveled slowly, heatedly over her. "Has anyone ever told you what a beautiful body you have?"

"It's been a while, but yes."

He gave her a wry smile. "Are you always honest?"

She nodded. "Sometimes without words, too."

She trailed a hand down her body, letting it linger over her sex. She parted herself and slid her finger inside the folds, liking the look of need in his eyes, how he watched her, wanted her…

A volt of sizzling electricity suddenly unleashed in the room.

He pressed her against the wall and, snaking an arm around her waist, pressed himself against her. She shuddered a groan at the sensation of their naked bodies connecting. Soft curves against hard muscles. Heat against heat.

A hand speared into her hair as his mouth claimed hers, his lips nibbling, licking, devouring.

She raised herself onto her toes and pressed herself against his hard member, positioning it against her cleft, *there*. Her breaths escaped in short pants as she gyrated slowly, hungrily against him, her body on fire with the wanting.

He grabbed her leg and hooked it over his hip. "Hold on."

As she wrapped her arms around his neck bracing the sole of her other foot against the floor, she heard the tell-tale sound of a condom wrapper opening. The quick movement of his unrolling the sheath over his erection.

Then he grasped her bottom and hauled her up, and she instinctively raised both legs to grip his hips, opening herself wide to him, realizing she'd never been this vulnerable to a man before yet going for it, all the same.

Tightening his arm around her waist for support, he glided his shaft into her. He growled as he sank deeper, his body shaking with restraint.

"It's okay," she whispered, sensations throbbing and roaring through her. "I want it, now."

He thrust fully into her, stretching her to capacity. She felt her insides closing around every inch of his thickness. With a final movement, he buried himself completely in her.

He worked her back and forth. Harder and harder, lifting her, forcing her down the length of his shaft.

She was vaguely aware of the bunched muscles under her grip, the salty taste of sweat on her lips, his mouth sucking the cry out of her.

Jarring explosions of pleasure suddenly rocked her, over and over. Her head fell back and she wailed his name.

He froze, then drove his climax into her with a roar.

An hour later, they lay in his living room in front of his fireplace, the light from the flickering flames rippling over their forms. Outside the windows, snow fell heavily, turning the dark sky gray.

Cecily wore Adam's sweater, which hit her mid-thigh. He'd tossed on a pair of black sweats. They were stretched out on an open sleeping bag, enjoying the heat from the fire while eating reheated pot roast and salad. On a side table were two glasses of ruby red Merlot.

"This roast is *fantastic*," Cecily said, taking another bite.

"I think you're just hungry," he teased, taking a sip of wine.

"I had this every Sunday growing up, so, trust me, I know excellent pot roast. Salad's great, too."

"Salad's salad."

She made a clucking noise. "I beg to differ. This has all kinds of chopped vegetables, croutons, grated cheese."

"Cecily," he said, looking at her warmly, "don't you cook?"

"Does making guacamole count?"

He laughed, liking their whimsy. Liked even more how she looked right now. Her hair mussed, his sweater hanging loosely on her, her face nearly devoid of make-up. She looked natural, relaxed, and he felt no small sense of male pride knowing he'd given her that certain afterglow.

"So who did the cooking in your family?"

"Grammy Sims, mostly. My mother was more one to open a can and heat it up, which is about my style."

"You sound like you miss them."

She paused. "I do. Especially my grandmother. We grew a lot closer when I lived with her during college."

"Why'd you move so far from home?"

She rolled her eyes. "Love. Or what I thought was love. I fell hard, and, next thing I knew, I was packed up and moving to Denver."

He waited. "And…?"

She chewed on a piece of carrot before answering. "And even though we were engaged, he thought he was still single."

The bum fooled around on her. Adam, for all his radio and book talk about babe baits and priming dates, didn't believe in screwing around behind someone's back. Relationships were challenging enough without that kind of crap.

"So what I've learned," she continued, "is I'll never uproot my life for someone again."

Can't blame her. "Why didn't you return to your family after that?"

"Actually, I was considering doing so after my lease ended on the Well Suited business space. Then Megan and I had our famous night of margaritas and the rest, as they say, is history."

She took a sip of wine, but not before he caught a flash of something in her eyes. He guessed the "history" had been a tougher challenge than relocating and dumping a dolt. She'd made money on her book, then lost most of it in that bad investment. Both her radio show and Well Suited business were struggling. And then there was this crazy TV reality show they were on.

One thing he knew for sure, she had guts to keep going despite the bad times.

"How about you?" she asked, spearing a piece of roast with her fork. "Your family's back east, right? Why did you move to Denver?"

"Got offered a management position after college, then I started Home Plate, penned my counter-attack to your book—"

She gave him a look.

"Despicable, I know," he said with a wink. "And the rest, as they say, is history."

"Ever think about moving back home?"

"Maybe the first year or two I was here, when I was more susceptible to bouts of homesickness. But my business is here, and my pals, so I'm pretty much a Denver boy now."

"Have you always been single?" She gave a small shake of her head. "Sorry. None of my business."

"You ask a lot of questions." He typically side

stepped discussions like this with women, but he felt surprisingly comfortable letting down his guard with Cecily. He trusted her, which, in his world, meant she was his friend. Friend and lover. He'd never had both with a woman before.

"I've had a few involvements, one that bordered on serious, otherwise I've been a single guy."

"But your dad and mom had a long marriage, right?"

"Long and happy, yes."

"You must miss him very much."

A pain sliced through his heart. "He was my father, but also my best friend."

Cecily watched Adam as he got up and busied himself poking the fire, turning a log. She couldn't help but wonder if Adam shied away from commitments because, on some subconscious level, he equated loving deeply with loss.

After a few minutes, he returned and sat next to her. "Warm enough?"

She nodded, nestling close and looking up into his face, half in golden incandescence from the firelight, half in mystifying shadow. She wondered about the shadowed facet of him. He was a complex, sensitive man who pretended to be simple and someday she'd ask him why.

But tonight, they'd talked enough. Words dogged their lives—words in their books, on their radio programs, even in teleprompters—and it was time to give it a rest.

He was staring into the fire, deep in thought, his

eyes gleaming golden in the firelight. Impulsively, she touched her finger to the sensitive spot between his nose and lip.

He cocked a questioning eyebrow and looked down at her, his solemn look crumbling.

She curled her hand around his neck and pulled him down to her.

Just the touch of her, the gardenia scent that would forevermore be her, made Adam's heart pound. And when her sweet, soft mouth took his he felt himself go crazy wanting her again.

He slipped down alongside her, taking her with him until they lay together on the cushy down of the sleeping bag. He studied her face. Had he ever noticed how her dark hair peaked appealingly on her forehead? Or how the color of her eyes reminded him of deep, rich chocolate?

He slipped his hand underneath the sweater and cupped her breast, felt her warmth. Leaning close to her ear, he released a lingering, hot breath, transmitting silently that he wanted to take this more gently, more slowly.

Her throaty murmur turned into a small gasp as he rotated a pebbled nipple between his fingers. He lightly kissed her cheeks and forehead, enjoying the sounds of enjoyment she made as he lightly tugged, stroked, kneaded her breasts.

When their eyes met, she gave him a smoldering look while silently mouthing his name. Adam... Adam...

He slid his hand down her middle, his fingers grazing her bare skin, her silken bare skin, until he reached her mound. She moaned softly as he moved his hand against her, parted her, then dipped into the silky folds.

Her breath caught raggedly in her throat. She tilted her pelvis, guiding him, asking him.

He slid one, then another finger, slowly inside her, marveling at her tight, wet warmth. He pushed deeper, more intimately, back and forth, until she emitted a sound of such intense pleasure he ached with the need to lose himself in her, physically and emotionally.

Then he withdrew his fingers and slid back up until he found her small feminine nub. He circled it, rubbed it, stroked it gently, so gently. She whimpered, straining for more, flexing her long, bare legs that gleamed like amber in the flickering firelight.

He increased the pressure ever so slightly, kept it steady, pressing and rubbing, until her body grew taut, stiffened, and when she cried out her pleasure he felt his own small corner of the universe was finally perfect.

He held her for a long moment afterward, brushing the hair back from her face, planting light kisses on her face and mouth. She finally opened her eyes. Gazing up at him, she smiled, trailing her fingertips across his face.

Such a simple gesture, yet it affected him profoundly. He couldn't recall when anyone had touched him so lovingly, so deeply. So much so, its intensity was nearly terrifying.

In emotional self-defense, he manacled her wrist and gently pulled her hand away. His breaths felt labored. Too hard for such a simple thing as the touch of a woman's hand to his cheek.

She gave him a look that said she understood more than he did. That she knew him.

That she loved him.

And that was when *he* knew, with a knowledge that bordered on visceral, that what truly mattered in life was this woman in his life. Releasing his hold on her wrist, he lifted her hand and kissed it.

She grinned, pulled her hand from his and ran her fingers over his chest, tickling, massaging, sliding her fingertips farther down until they reached the waistband of his sweatpants.

She gave him a sly, inviting look as her hand glided over the waistband and onto the bulge beneath the soft cotton material. She curled her fingers around the hard swelling and gave it a long, slow squeeze.

A breath exploded from his lungs and he rolled her over. He tugged off his sweatpants and reached for something. A small packet glinted in the firelight and she hoped he had plenty more of those babies planted around his place. He rolled it down the length of his shaft and positioned himself over her, giving her such an intense, smoldering look, she couldn't open her legs fast enough.

She felt his erection part her, slide slowly in until

he filled her completely. Holding onto his buttocks, she shifted a little to accommodate him, gasping when he thrust even deeper.

As he rocked his hips with deep, firm strokes she looked into his face, thinking how masculine, fierce, *sexual* he looked.

Then his strokes intensified, driving long and hard, and she stopped thinking altogether. She heard herself moaning, the sound rising in pitch, Adam's unholy grin looking down at her, then suddenly all the throbbing, pounding, pulsing inside her hitched to a still plateau…

She blasted off the edge of the world in an explosion of white-hot heat as wave after wave of ecstasy hit her. She dug her fingers into his butt, pulling him in even deeper, and rode him, hard.

He slammed into her, drops of sweat rolling down his face, until, after impaling her with one final thrust, he groaned her name and she felt the powerful contractions that signaled his release.

He tumbled off to the side of her, and pulled her close again.

They lay there for a long time until their bodies cooled and their heaving breaths quieted. Adam tossed part of the sleeping bag over their bodies, and they cuddled while listening to the crackling fire and watching the falling snow outside the window.

Cecily thought how those two elements, fire and snow, were like she and Adam. People had thought one would beat, or destroy, the other. Fire melting snow; water dousing fire. But just the opposite had turned out to be true.

Their worlds could exist side by side, complementing each other. One providing warmth, the other offering solace.

Together, in their own unique way, creating a haven.

CHAPTER ELEVEN

CHIRP-DE-CHIRP. Chirp-de-chirp.

Cecily groggily rubbed her cheek against the sheet, catching a lingering scent that was almost familiar...deliciously, uniquely familiar...

Chirp-de-chirp. Chirp-de-chirp.

She yawned, fumbled behind her for the phone on her nightstand. She touched something warm, firm, sprinkled with hair, thought for a moment it was her cat Bob until her foggy state cleared a little and she realized she was touching a few silky strands, not fur.

Definitely not her cat Bob.

Chirp-de-chirp.

Not the ring of her cell phone, either. She squinted open one eye. Pale winter light sifted through a bank of windows that offered an endless view of sky. An entertainment center crowded the opposite wall. Barbells lay in the corner on a honey-colored oak floor.

Not her room, either.

Chirp-de—

"I got it," rumbled a deep male voice. "Hullo?"

She turned her head. Her hand lay on a naked male chest attached to a sleepy-faced Adam.

"Ya don't say," he said groggily into the cell, cocking a grin at Cecily.

Memories of last night came searing back. She and Adam stumbling into the house. Wild, can't-wait sex right there in the hallway. Later, more lovemaking on a sleeping bag in front of the fire. In her mind, she ticked off the number of orgasms she'd had. One, two, three. If she recalled correctly, three had a four and a five in there, too.

The man was a beast.

"Cool," Adam said. He reached over and tousled her hair.

God. What does my hair look like? This was the downside of having curly hair—after a night of unleashed sex followed by tumble-into-bed sleep, her hair could have mushroomed into something with a life of its own. She glanced around the room again. Just like a man to not have a mirror handy.

He punched a button on the cell, tossed it onto a nightstand, and turned to her.

"That was the producer of *Marriage Material...or Misfortune?*

"He called *you*?" She'd never got a call from the producer directly, except after she'd forwarded that wardrobe requirements memo. Which could only mean one thing. Adam won last night's date.

She felt a twinge of remorse that it hadn't been her, but it passed surprisingly quickly. What hit her hardest was the incredible sense of relief that the stressful dating series was over. No, not merely relief. *Liberation.* Finally, she could get back to living her normal life, figure out what to do with Well Suited, figure out the next steps with the radio program....

Figure out what she and Adam were really about.

That one had slipped in. No, a bad idea. If she'd learned anything in her twenty-four years, it was dangerous to contemplate the what-ifs in the throes of post-coital, foggy-brained passion.

Instead she gave him her best sincere smile. "Congratulations."

Adam looked surprised, then grinned. "No, honey, *you* won last night's date."

She felt as though she'd just taken a swan dive out his tenth-story window.

"Me?" Her breath hitched as she flashed back on being late to the hockey game, the glob of unsightly mustard on her jacket, running like a prison escapee toward the exit. "Why would more people have voted for *me*?"

"Well, speaking for myself, you made quite an impression when you walked in, looking drop-dead gorgeous. Plus, you give back as good as you get. And I don't mean after we got to my place, although you were terrific there, too." He gave her a look that made her heart somersault.

"We're, uh..." she fumbled for words as she stared into those lethal blue eyes "...we're going to have another date."

A fifth date. Another competition.

Her heart sank. Yes, yes, there was the grand prize money, the PR opportunities, the growing fame that really wasn't feeling all that great. She'd already weathered the limelight with her and Megan's book, the radio show, now this TV extravaganza, but all that didn't take away the fact she was fundamentally a private person. Hardly someone accustomed to total strangers commenting on her private life, asking how Adam kissed. What else would they ask prying questions about?

"I have a confession," she finally said.

His eyebrows raised.

"I wish you'd won last night."

"Cecily!"

"I mean it. I didn't quit because it wasn't fair to you, and I won't threaten to quit again for that same reason, but I wish it was over. I want my life back."

He gathered her into his arms, making a soft shushing sound as though comforting a child.

"I'd have voted for you last night," she continued. They were each allowed a vote, by calling the 800-number or logging onto the marriagematerial.com site and filling out the form, even given the leniency of doing so by one a.m., rather than the midnight cut-off given to everyone else.

"And it would have been an honest vote, too," she said, "and not me trying to worm out of a fifth date."

"Cecily," he murmured, cuddling her, "you're tired, that's all."

"No, I mean it. You would have earned my vote because the perfect boyfriend provides spontaneous adventures, and you certainly did that when you encouraged our running from fans, then grabbing that taxi, then…" *Asking me to come home with you.*

She smiled to herself, savoring the memory of that taxi ride, the vulnerability she'd seen in his face. And later, the touches of care he'd shown by making dinner, bringing out the sleeping bag, opening up a little about his father.

Opening up his heart a little.

She cupped Adam's face with her hand, swallowing hard as a sudden emotion took hold of her. Screw the danger of post-coital contemplation, she wanted to know—was this a passing fancy for him, or something lasting? Or even something that had the *possibility* of being lasting? A little voice inside her head chided herself for wanting to know. After all, she was an independent woman, a self-starter.

But life wasn't always about standing alone. She knew from collaborating with Megan, or living with her family, that sometimes the greater strength came from sharing. And since when was it nobler to go the we'll-always-have-Paris route when maybe she wanted to stay in Paris for the rest of her life. With Adam. Hell, she was even willing to learn to cook.

A small sob escaped her lips.

"Oh, sweetheart," Adam murmured, holding her closer. "I'd have voted for you, too. In my book, the perfect girlfriend also loves spontaneous adventures, isn't afraid to divulge who she is, has interests that are uniquely her own."

When she didn't respond, he pulled back slightly and looked into her eyes. "Anyway, it doesn't matter if we'd voted because we'd just have cancelled out each other."

She nodded, forcing herself to return to reality. It was better this way, staying in the here and now, not anticipating the future.

"Right," she agreed. "We'd have cancelled each other out."

She looked down at his chest, took in his scent, felt that familiar, hot need tingling all over her. "Now that there's a date five," she murmured, "we have to be on our best behavior this next week. Which means no more fraternizing."

His hand trailed a path over the jut of her hip. "Is that what this is called?"

"Yes." She smiled. "The best fraternizing I've ever had, too, by the way."

She gasped as his palm smoothed over her heated skin, swept down her body, igniting every nerve ending, taking her to that place just the two of them shared. He whispered dark, thrilling things into her ear as his fingers stroked, rubbed, cajoled her body to be his lover. And she opened herself to him, greedy for their lovemaking.

Paris, after all, was a state of mind.

* * *

A week later, at six-thirty p.m., Cecily stood inside the lobby of the super-chic, five-star Palace hotel in downtown Denver, the setting for the fifth and, thank God, *last* date.

She fumbled for her cigarette pack. She'd been smoking more this week, didn't care, and nobody who wanted to live and tell about it had better try to stop her.

Bradley, wearing a loose-fitting cream-colored suit with a wide turquoise tie, strolled toward her with the usual entourage in his wake.

Just as he went to air-kiss her, she stopped him.

"Bradley, there's something I have to tell you."

He looked at her, his beady little eyes blinking. "What, darling?"

"I don't…" *want to be here hate being here and by the way I haven't fraternized in five days thanks to this damn show…*

"What?" he asked, looking worried. His mood had trickled down to his entourage, who stared at Cecily with big, concerned looks.

She cleared her throat. "I don't want you calling me Felicity anymore."

He did a double take. "Why?"

"Because it's not my name."

"What is?"

"Cecily."

"Ce-cil-y," he repeated, as though tasting a foreign food. He looked back at his entourage. "Did you know her name is Ce-cil-y?"

A few shrugged, one nodded yes.

Bradley looked back at her. "Darling, I'm so sorry. Is that why you've been acting so oddly?"

She looked around the room, debating how much hysteria to share with him. "Maybe it's this place. It's so uncomfortably ritzy—"

"No, not tonight," he interrupted. "I meant, all along."

She gave him a long look, thinking how she so *didn't* need to hear that before launching into tonight's live reality date with millions of people watching.

"You have nothing to worry about," he continued, stepping back to look her over. "Because you look absolutely fabulous tonight. Love the skirt, those understated pumps, and that blue jacket with the piping and dash-of-red scarf, all exquisite."

So what if she'd been odd? She looked fabulous. Life was, after all, about give and take.

"You got the script?" he asked.

"Three days ago."

"Fabulous. As you're aware we'll start filming here, in the lobby atrium. A musician will be playing the baby grand in the background as you introduce the location. One slight change. Rather than have you and Adam be on a generic historical tour of the hotel, it'll be a *Lovers' Ghost Tour* instead."

"Lovers' Ghost Tour?"

Roger bounded up, shoved a piece of paper in front of Bradley, who scanned it and nodded his approval. Roger bounded off again.

"Yes," Bradley said. "Seems there are lovers who

died in the hotel, one or two in this very lobby, who haunt the place. The Lovers' Ghost Tour is one of several the hotel offers, and the producers thought it'd be perfect for the last date."

Why? Was the network hoping she or Adam would lose it and attempt a double homicide?

"Remember the teleprompter will always be nearby, and good luck."

As he walked away Delores appeared in a cloud of White Shoulders traced with cigarette smoke. She wore a festive red ensemble with sparkling red-and-white earrings. Her make-up looked more colorful, more artfully applied.

"You look wonderful, dear," she said, brushing at the sleeve on Cecily's jacket.

"You, too! Va-va-voom!"

A shy smile curved the older woman's lips. "I'm going out for martinis after the show tonight."

"Oh?"

"One of the lighting technicians. We've known each other forever."

Cecily checked out the crew. "Which one?"

"The Kirk Douglas look-alike in the yellow crew-neck."

"Cute. He keeps sneaking peeks at you." Cecily looked back at Delores. "I think he likes you."

"We'll see," Delores said coyly.

"First date?"

"Yes." She looked at Cecily. "And you?"

"Me what?"

"You and Adam…" She fussed with the lapel of Cecily's jacket, letting the question hang.

"We've had a real date. Well, sort of." Heat filled her cheeks at the memory of the night they'd shared. They hadn't seen each other since then because they were abiding by the network's condition they not fraternize. Which was a good thing because they'd become the media's darlings, with reporters trying to sniff out any snippets of juicy news before the last big date.

Cecily lifted her cigarette, tried to light it, but her hand shook too much.

Delores pulled a silver lighter out of her pocket, lit the cigarette for her. "Everything will work out."

The tobacco sizzled, Cecily took a drag and released it. "My mind sort of wants to win," she finally said, "but my heart isn't into it."

"Finally realized you're in love with the guy, huh?"

"I didn't say that."

"Didn't need to." Delores gave her a hug. "If life were always perfect, what would we appreciate?"

Cecily was still pondering that comment a few minutes later as the make-up girl dabbed at her face. Life had definitely had its imperfections this past year-plus, and Cecily was trying to figure out what she appreciated because of that.

After losing money, she could certainly appreciate its value. After losing Megan as her co-host on their radio show, she *really* appreciated anybody who could entertain under pressure. After losing the business space for her Well Suited business, she appreciated any orders generated from her web site. Orders that had picked up nicely since the museum date when she'd started wearing—and, once, flashing—her Well Suited designs. She smiled to herself, thinking of the orders for a "flashing jacket" she'd received since then.

She looked across the room at Adam, who looked dashing in a blue sweater underneath a brown sports coat that matched his hair. He looked at her, and even from across the room she could feel their chemistry. So volatile, she swore it could incinerate the air around them.

She thought about their books, *The Perfect Boyfriend* and *The Perfect Girlfriend*. Funny to think how, in the beginning, they'd each been so self-righteous about their rules, so judgmental about each other. She'd viewed him as a cretin, he'd viewed her as—what had he and his buds called her? Oh, right, a librarian dominatrix.

And now they were lovers.

She didn't want to compete with this man. Pour her energy into outwitting, out-maneuvering him. She didn't want the stress, the hype, the going for the jugular anymore.

No, she'd play it fair tonight. If she couldn't be herself and win, then what was she winning by being someone else?

She took another puff, thinking how two imperfect people had learned to appreciate each other.

Across the room, Adam watched Cecily pacing

and smoking. After that steel-melting look they'd shared, all he wanted to do was be making love with her, not war. In a perfect world, he wished this could be a tie. Split it down the middle, a nice twelve-plus grand each, no winner, no loser.

Problem was, a little over twelve thousand wouldn't be sufficient for Cecily to ramp up her business, nor would it cover what he needed for a men's recreational baseball team.

One of them needed to be the winner to get what they wanted.

Which made him realize, what he really wanted was for Cecily to be that winner.

Sugar Megs, who'd topped her pastel tie-dyed shirt with a pink blazer, had an intense look as she listened to her headset. After a quick nod to Bradley, who was hunched over a monitor while talking to a technician, she held up five fingers.

"Five…"

Cecily sucked in a deep breath.

"Four…"

She glanced at Adam, off camera, who winked at her.

"Three…"

Delores, a cigarette in one hand, held up her other with her fingers crossed.

"Two…"

This is it. Liberation is an hour away.

On one, Sugar Megs held up her index finger and pointed at Cecily.

"Welcome to date number five," she said, looking into the camera. Piano music tinkled in the background. The air was scented with evergreen from the gigantic Christmas tree in the middle of the atrium.

"Tonight we're at Denver's historical Palace, a grande dame hotel who, for more than a century, has played host to presidents, princesses, kings and queens."

She walked a few steps across one of the oriental rugs that dotted the marble floor and stood next to a potted palm decorated with twinkling lights.

"Tonight, we're starting the date in the eight-story atrium at the core of the hotel, decorated this year with a forty-foot tree that soars toward the antique stained-glass ceiling."

She gestured upward as the camera panned past the gold Mexican-onyx walls, up the tree with its hundreds of red bows and sparkling lights, all the way to the stained-glass ceiling that glowed yellow, orange, purple, green.

Cecily took advantage of the moment to glance at Adam, who was looking at her as though she, not the elegant million-dollar décor, was the beauty in the room. If the man was trying to play an aggressive game, he was failing sorely.

She heard Bradley clearing his throat.

"Tonight," she said, looking back into the camera,

"we'll be taking a special tour of lovers' ghosts here in the Brown Palace…"

Over the following ten or so minutes, she read the script, the extras took their places, the tour began. She felt strangely calm, probably because she'd made her choice to just be herself, not fight for the votes. Adam seemed strangely calm, too, although she wasn't sure why.

Bradley, on the other hand, was losing it. Once he held up a sign that said, "Conflict, please!"

She and Adam ignored it.

After the commercial break, they were straggling a group of extras as the Palace tour guide—a woman in her twenties dressed in a conservative black suit—started another ghost story, one about the female apparition in a corset who floated over visitors' beds.

"The rumor," said the tour guide, "is the ghost is one of the prostitutes who worked across the street in a bordello that, back in the eighteen nineties, was connected to the hotel via a secret tunnel."

Adam glanced at Cecily, wondering what she'd look like in a corset. She caught his look, and gave him a smile that said pretty good, thank you. He'd never shared a telepathic moment with a woman before. If they could connect with a hot thought, God help them when their bodies got together again.

As her eyes sparkled knowingly at him he felt his heart trip in his chest. Was this what falling in love was like?

He'd witnessed it, certainly, in his parents. They'd

darn near glowed whenever they'd been together, even after thirty-odd years of marriage. He couldn't count the number of times he'd walk into a room and they'd be sneaking a kiss. When his father died, his mother's world had crumpled. He and his brother had grieved, too, but whenever he looked in his mom's eyes it was as though a light had gone out.

He didn't want that for himself. He didn't want to lose someone who'd been such a vital part of himself that when she left, he'd never be whole again.

He looked at Cecily and her twinkling eyes, that impish grin, and his heart tripped again. And he wondered if falling in love was fated, not a choice. If maybe sharing a lifetime was worth the inevitability.

The tour guide launched into another story.

"Three years ago while doing this very tour," she said, gesturing to a room door, "I told the story of Eliza Donald, a female resident who, after a disastrous affair, literally became a hermit in this room for the rest of her life, finally dying of old age and a broken heart. Two hours after my tour ended, the switchboard of the hotel was flooded with calls from this room, but every time the operator answered, there was only static. What was odd was that the room was being remodeled at the time and everything in the room had been stripped, including the phone lines."

Some of the extras, and Cecily, gasped.

"This continued for the next two times I did the tour. I'd tell Eliza's story, the switchboard would be flooded with calls, more static. I told the manager of the hotel I would be discontinuing Eliza's story from the next tour. The calls stopped."

The tour guide cast a look at the group. "Which makes one wonder if unrequited love continues into eternity."

Cecily shuddered, grabbed Adam's hand.

And at that moment, he had his answer. If love continued into eternity, seemed kinda silly living a life anticipating loss. Out of range of the camera, he raised Cecily's hand to his lips, kissed it.

Bradley, talking into his headset, paced to a spot where they could see him. He made a cutting motion across his neck.

Adam released her hand.

With an exasperated roll of his eyes, Bradley gave the go-ahead for the camera to turn on them again.

And Adam saw his opportunity to help Cecily win.

"I have trouble believing that ghost called the switchboard," he said loudly. "No woman ever made a call and let static speak for her." One of the male extras snickered.

Cecily stared at Adam for a long moment. "I can't believe you said that."

"Said what, babe?"

"Said—" Babe? Since when had he started referring to her as a babe again? Was he baiting her?

Oh, no-o-o. She wasn't going into combat again. No more Clash of the Perfects or Beauty Battles the Beast.

Then a realization dawned on her. This wasn't the

Stud Man. This was Adam *pretending* to be the Stud Man. She knew him well enough to recognize a sparkle of mischief in his eyes.

Oh, yes. She got his game. Or, to put it more accurately, how he was *throwing* his game. By going the Cro-Mag route again, he would make sure women would vote for her. He wanted her to win, to rebuild her business.

Which was the ultimate rule in her and Megan's book—that a truly perfect boyfriend would do anything to make his woman happy.

She loved him for it, but that didn't mean she wanted him to purposely lose. It didn't feel right.

Except…

She could throw her game, too. Then this date would be fun because they'd both want the best for the other.

Plus, it would make Bradley crazy, which was a good enough reason in itself.

After another commercial break, Adam and Cecily were looking over a section of wrought-iron banister at the lobby several floors below. Maybe she'd felt nervous before the date had begun, but now she felt relaxed. Well, almost. Standing this close to him had her insides jangling. From the rise and fall of his chest, he was jangling, too.

"At that very spot," the tour guide said, pointing to an area near the massive granite fireplace, "Mr James entered the lobby with his gun drawn, looking for his wife's lover, Mr Andersen. The two men encountered each other. Shots rang out. When Mrs James entered the lobby, she found both her husband and her lover dead."

"Two with one stone," said Cecily loudly. "Women don't often get lucky like that."

The group turned so quiet, all that could be heard was the faint whir of machinery and the murmur of voices and laughter from the downstairs bar. At that moment, a ruddy-faced man staggered out of the bar, looked up and waved. Cecily ignored him, turned back to the tour group. Some of the women extras in the group frowned at her. Bradley stared at her as though she'd finally snapped.

As did Adam. For a moment, anyway. Then he got a look in his eyes that said he'd caught on.

Let the *real* games begin.

"So," he said, directing his attention to the guide, "do all three of them haunt the hotel?"

"Actually," she said, adjusting her glasses, "people have only seen the men, not her."

"Lucky men," said Adam.

"Or lucky her," countered Cecily.

And so they continued. Adam faking it as a sexist male, Cecily faking it as the anti-Adam. Each of them hearing the votes piling in for the other.

The tour group headed down the staircase, stepping onto the white marble floor of the lobby. As they passed over an old heating grate Cecily suddenly felt a blast of heat. Her skirt blew up.

She slapped her hands against the material, forcing down the wayward skirt, then stood there stiffly, her face hot with embarrassment. God, if only she'd worn her granny panties instead of those skimpy black thong undies.

Adam flashed her a look of commiseration, even as his eyes twinkled. Oh, yeah, she knew what he was thinking. That moment of humiliation just bought more empathy votes from women, as well as more from men who'd vote for any exposed part of a woman's anatomy.

Sugar Megs was making a winding-up sign, indicating the show would be wrapping soon.

The date was almost over. No more surreal dating experiences, no games, just the real world. Cecily felt as though she were finally releasing a breath she'd been holding for weeks when the man she'd seen earlier staggering out of the downstairs bar ambled up to her.

"Nice shot," he said lasciviously. "Care to stand over that grate again?"

"I don't appreciate your suggestion," she said, biting back what she *really* wanted to say. "Please leave."

His descriptive, terse response had Bradley scrambling for the five-second delay.

Adam stepped between her and the man. "You heard the lady. Leave her alone."

"She doesn't belong to you," the man snarled.

"No, she belongs only to herself. So apologize, and leave."

"Here's my apology." The man tossed a swing.

Adam blocked it with his arm, his other fist cold-cocking the guy with a sickening, bone-crunching sound. The man staggered back a few steps before sinking heavily to a sitting position on the floor, a stunned look on his face.

"Cut!" yelled Bradley.

CHAPTER TWELVE

CECILY FLICKED on the light switch. The ceiling globe came to life, lighting up her apartment living room, much of it covered in swatches of material, patterns, scissors and other sewing paraphernalia.

Taking off her coat, she stomped her snow-covered boots on a piece of carpet that doubled for a rug. Tossing the coat onto the table that held her industrial sewing machine, she checked the wall clock. Twelve-fifteen. Briskly rubbing her fingers, which she'd kept jammed in her coat pockets on the brisk walk from the shuttle to her apartment, she headed to the kitchen.

Making margaritas in the dead of winter was what separated the women from the girls.

Bob, who'd been lying on a corner of the couch, jumped down and followed her, emitting an elongated craggy meow.

"Since you asked, tonight's date number five went fine, although it ended on a testosterone high when Adam punched out some drunk who accosted me."

Bob's short tail twitched.

"You guys like those macho theatrics, don't you?"

Meow.

"I love our conversations, Bob, although I'm fairly certain all you're really saying is, 'Feed me, feed me.'" After pouring him a saucer of milk, she dug out the ice-cube tray from her freezer, which resembled a miniature frozen tundra. One of these days, she'd really get around to defrosting it. Which she'd been saying for a couple of months now.

Beep de beep. Beep de beep.

She looked around for her cell phone, fairly certain its ring originated from behind a barricade of cereal boxes and canisters at the end of the kitchen counter.

Beep de beep. Beep de beep.

She tossed the ice tray into the sink. Shoving aside a box, she spied the phone and picked it up.

"Hello?"

"Sweetpea," said Theodore. "I've been trying to call you for several hours."

"Left my cell at home." She reached into the cereal box, grabbed a handful. "I ended up staying at the Brown Palace forever after the date ended." She nibbled on the crunchy, sweet cereal.

"Why?"

She swallowed, headed to the ice tray. "Oh, let's see. After the police took my statement about Adam punching out that drunk, and Adam got written up for disorderly conduct, we went to the Ship's Tavern bar in the hotel for the wrap party, which was a mob scene." She dumped some ice into the blender.

"Was the mayor there?"

"Smiling and shaking everyone's hand." She rummaged in a cabinet, retrieved the tequila. "I kept trying to leave, but every time I did somebody wanted to talk, or request an interview. One guy was trying to talk me into a business venture to make bumper stickers." Shaking her head, she poured the liquor into the blender. "Finally, I sneaked out and grabbed the shuttle, which was a *huge* mistake. I was more famous on the shuttle than I'd been at the party." She checked the level, shrugged, glugged more in. "Who'd have thought so many people watched *Marriage Material...or Misfortune?*"

"Reality shows are hot."

"It's weird having total strangers act as though they know you, though. You wouldn't *believe* some of the questions they ask."

"You mean like, how much do you weigh?"

"That's nothing."

"What happened to the drunk guy?"

"Police hauled him off to detox."

"They arrest Adam?"

She laughed, grabbing a packet of instant margarita mix. "No, they only wrote him a ticket. One of the cops was even laughing about it. That was one expensive punch, I tell you. Hold on, blender time."

She turned it on, counted to four as the ice clattered, the machine whirred. She flipped the off switch.

"I'm back." She poured some of the frothy concoction into a glass, took a sip. "Excellent."

"Good."

Silence.

She frowned, headed into the living room. "What's up?"

"Sweetpea…" His voice trailed off.

"That's the saddest sounding sweetpea I've ever heard." She sat at the end of the couch, took another sip. Bad news was coming, she could feel it. "You and David all right?"

"Oh, we're great. Planning a trip to New Orleans soon."

Everybody seemed to be pairing up. Delores and Kirk. Theo and David. She hadn't had a chance to say two words to Adam after the date had ended, wondered if he'd stayed at the party.

"What's wrong?" she asked.

"You lost tonight."

It wasn't as if she had her heart set on winning, but all the same something fluttered and sank in her chest.

She glanced again at the clock. Almost twelve-thirty. Of course, the votes for date number five were in. Typically, she got "the call" first thing the following morning, but the TV show was probably releasing the stats immediately tonight.

Bye-bye funding for Well Suited.

Theo made a little strangled noise. "I'm sorry."

"Me, too." She took a sip. "Truth is, I feel bad, yes, but not devastated. After all, I was ready to toss in the towel before date four, remember? I'd reached a point where I knew I could give up the money to have some peace of mind."

"Yes, I remember."

"And tonight's date was actually fun because Adam and I played instead of battled."

Theo choked back a sob.

"Theo, please don't be sad."

"But I didn't tell you the worst part. You lost by one vote. One *measly* vote."

Ouch. Okay, it hurt a bit more knowing she'd come that close. She took a mondo sip of her margarita, letting its tangy chill temper the sting.

"I voted for you, darling. So did David."

"Well, bottom line, that's what counts." She even meant it. Sort of.

"Meet for coffee in the morning?"

She thought again about the strangers who'd pelted her with questions on the shuttle tonight. "I think I need to steer clear of public places for a while." She wondered how long this scrutiny would continue. Was she going to have to wear disguises when she left her home?

"I wanted us to get together," Theo continued, his voice choking up again, "because there's something else I need to tell you."

Even more? From the sound of his voice, this wasn't good news, either. She downed another sip, preparing herself for the next wave.

"The radio show—" a loud sniff "…has pulled the

plug. I'm so sorry, sweetpea. I didn't know they were planning this until just a few minutes ago."

She knew KNOA hadn't been pleased with *The Perfect Boyfriend* ratings, although she'd hoped the hike in listeners with her appearances in *Marriage Material...or Misfortune?* had helped. Guess again.

"Who are they replacing me with?"

Bob meowed.

Theodore sighed heavily. "Some former model who's written a book titled *How to Marry a Millionaire*—like, hello, that's so passé—and she's going to prove her approach by dating a bunch of millionaires and marrying one."

"Gee, guess Megan and I really raised the communal consciousness a notch."

"She's the flavor of the month. What can I say?"

"I miss Grammy Sims," Cecily suddenly murmured, thinking how all the signs seemed to be pointing for her to return home. She had no job, had lost a big chunk of funding for her struggling business, plus she'd have to wear disguises every time she left her apartment.

She heard a light knocking at her door. "Sounds like I have company."

"Well, it's not me."

She had to laugh despite their sobering conversation. "No, Theo," she said, heading to the door, "I don't think you'd stand on the other side of my door, talking to me on your cell."

"I would if I thought I'd pissed you off."

"Well, you never have. Much." She looked through the peephole. There stood Adam, snowflakes scattered on his brown hair, cheeks. Her heart pumped a little faster.

"Gotta go," she whispered.

"Who is it?" Theo asked.

"Adam," she whispered, unlocking the dead bolt.

"Are you two…?"

"Yes."

Theodore gasped. "And you didn't tell me?"

"Look, gotta go." She scraped open the chain lock.

"I want a detailed report first thing tomorrow—"

"Yes, yes." She punched the End button, opened the door.

Her heart lurched at the sight of Adam. He looked lethally sophisticated in a long black wool coat with a knit scarf wound around his neck. Stray licks of light glinted off his wind-blown hair and ruddy cheeks. Add that simmering look in his blue eyes and it was all she could do to open her mouth and form coherent words.

"Hi," she whispered.

"Hi."

His deep voice rumbled all the way down her spine.

He looked questioningly at her for a long moment and she felt herself go soft inside. God, the man *exuded* virility. She shifted from one foot to the other, aware her breath was growing just the tiniest bit ragged.

"Uh, may I come in?"

"Oh!" She quickly stepped back. "Sorry."

As he stepped inside she caught his scent, one that would be forevermore seared into her brain.

She closed the door and turned, watched him pull off his black leather gloves and tuck them into his coat pockets.

He looked up, his eyes crinkling with a smile. "Didn't have a chance to talk to you tonight."

"Well, things got busy with the police, and then that wall-to-wall party." She looked at his hand, thinking of the punch he'd planted on that jerk. "Are you all right?"

He shrugged, flexed the fingers. "No big deal." He dropped his hand, took a step toward her. "But I didn't come here to talk about that. I wanted first to tell you that I've missed you."

He gathered her into his arms, and she felt his breath hot in her ear.

"God…I…missed…you," he growled.

His hand tangled in her hair and pulled her head back. He made a low, hungry sound deep in his throat as he widened his mouth over hers, and then she was lost in a kiss that made her mouth burn with fire. Electricity shot through her, followed by a building joy that crowded out her thoughts and melded every touch, smell, taste into a singular, golden moment where time itself stopped. No before, no after, just now, this man, this kiss…oh, God, this kiss…

She was vaguely aware of his gently pushing her away. Surfacing from her foggy haze, she opened her eyes, looked into his face. He exhaled sharply, shook his head, looked at the ground, looked at her.

He raked a hand through his hair. "That was…"

He felt it, too. "Amazing," she whispered.

"Unbelievable. I've been waiting all night to do that."

"I've been waiting all week."

"I've been waiting since the beginning of time."

A laugh caught in her throat. "Are we still competing? Well, I—I love you," she blurted.

He did a double take, blinked. "This is all happening so fast."

Outside could be heard the slush of cars driving through snow. Someone laughed. A horn honked.

"It's okay," she finally said, breaking their silence. She mentally kicked herself. Didn't she, of all people, know better than to get swept away in a moment of passion? That was so *not* the time to make decisions, much less make certain statements. Especially the kind that could give a man instant cardiac arrest.

"I love you, too," he said.

She stilled, letting the words sink in. "Oh, good," she whispered, her heart floating, singing, dancing. "I didn't want to be the only one."

He chuckled, giving her a look that bored right down to her most secret self.

She'd once thought she was the one who saw through his veneer, but, looking into his eyes, she realized how deeply he knew her as well. Knew her fears, worries, hopes, dreams. Knew how all those feelings got jumbled up inside her, sometimes came out the wrong way, or awkwardly, but he understood why.

It gave her a sense of acceptance she'd never experienced with a man. It was a tremendous relief to not have to be anything but herself, imperfections and all, in order to be loved.

Adam unbuttoned the top few buttons of his coat, gave her a smile. "I'd actually wanted to talk about a few other things first, but nothing wrong with working from the top down."

"I know I lost tonight's date, Adam."

He paused, then nodded slowly. "And yet you still kissed me like that?"

"All's fair in love and war," she said with a shrug, acting more nonchalant than she felt.

"Tonight wasn't war," he said solemnly. "Fake war, maybe, but I sensed we wanted each other to win. In fact, I think you had it nailed until I slugged the guy. That over-the-top Hollywood ending was what pushed an extra vote or two my way."

He'd given this a lot of thought, she could tell. And he felt badly about it.

"It's nothing you did wrong," she said. "In fact, maybe it's part of everything you're doing right. Your radio show is hot, your book is hot, I bet Home Plate will be bursting at the seams with new clientele, plus you've won the twenty-five grand. You know how they say the universe shows you a sign if you're headed in the right direction? I think you're getting sign after sign."

Until this moment, she hadn't really thought about that as it pertained to herself. Not so long ago,

Adam had asked why she hadn't returned home after her relationship had crashed, when she'd found herself living alone in Denver without family or community.

She'd said she'd been waiting for her business lease to run out, but, looking back, she should have cut her losses then and gone home. Instead she'd stuck it out, but it'd been uphill all the way. Tenacious being her middle name, she'd forged on despite the bad investment, the struggling radio show and jacket business, and now losing the TV competition.

Maybe she'd been ignoring the universe's big neon sign plunked right in front of her.

"I think it's time I go home," she said quietly.

He looked stunned. "Cecily—"

"I'm serious. Plus, it's getting increasingly uncomfortable in Denver with total strangers pumping me for details about my personal life. I need a break, a chance to regroup, rebuild Well Suited at my own pace. Plus I miss my family."

He reached out, caught her hands in his.

"Marry me. I'll be your family."

Her breath caught in her throat. "Now things are going too fast for *me*."

Adam stared at her, his heart and mind racing. "We're good together. We've been through more in five dates than most people have in a year of dating. Let's just do away with the rest of it, go straight for home plate. Let's get rings, plan the day, go someplace warm for our honeymoon—"

"Adam…"

"What, honey?"

"When I said I love you, I meant it. But I can't fit my life into someone else's again. Especially not when everything's up in the air—how do I know who I am, or even what I truly want, if I just try to merge into someone else's world?"

He heard the words, but couldn't stop the momentum of his thoughts and desires. "You could move into my place. We'll make my guest bedroom into your work area. I'll ask if you can do a guest spot or two on my radio show."

She shook her head sadly. "Adam, listen to me, please. I can't just move into your world—where does mine go? That's what I did with another man when I relocated to Denver, and I learned the hard way that worlds don't always blend, sometimes parts of one get fragmented or lost. That's what happened to me and I swore I'd never do it again."

His throat tightened. "I need you, Cecily."

He'd done what he'd once sworn he'd never do. He'd fallen in love, made himself vulnerable, opened himself up to every damn arrow of hurt and rejection and loss. She was holding firm, wouldn't give in no matter what he pleaded or promised—he could see that. *Knew* that.

Those thoughts had barely crossed his mind when another followed.

Despite the pain, it didn't mean opening himself up to love hadn't been worth it. Every single moment.

And that was when he saw the parallel with his father. Through death his old man had had to leave, and it had hurt like hell for those left behind. But that didn't mean the time they'd shared hadn't been worth it. Every single moment.

Adam paused, gathered his thoughts. "If you'd won the twenty-five grand, you'd have stayed in Denver, right?"

"Probably. Maybe. The money would have made it easier."

He pulled out his cell phone, punched in a number. "It's not one o'clock yet." He handed the phone to her. "Vote for yourself."

She gave a start of surprise. "I can't do that."

"We'll both be winners this way."

"It's crazy. You'll lose half your prize money."

"I want to support you in your new life. This is my going-away gift, twelve thousand, five hundred dollars for you to buy inventory, get settled, maybe even do something nice for yourself."

He knew she desperately needed the money. One more nudge…

"Trust me, twelve thousand and change is plenty for a bunch of ageing jocks to start their own baseball team."

She took the phone and voted for herself.

Adam took back the phone…and voted for her, too.

She looked at him, stunned, as he dropped the phone back into his coat pocket.

"You didn't tell me you hadn't voted yet."

Adam cupped the side of her face, stroked her cheekbone with his thumb. Even if she had asked, he would have lied.

"Are you doing this to—?" She bit off the rest of the sentence.

He frowned. "Win you back?"

She pursed her lips.

"What, you think we're still using the rules from our books to manipulate each other?" He gave his head a shake. "Low blow, Cecily."

She started to respond, but he cut her off.

"I've spent years avoiding the pain of loss," he said, "but now I realize avoiding it means living only half a life." He lowered his head and dropped a heart-breakingly sweet kiss on her lips. "You know, I may have won more tonight than you did."

His cell rang. He answered, nodded, his lips pressing into a thin smile.

He ended the call, looked at Cecily. "That was Bradley. I forgot that, after the last show, viewers had a one-time vote on whether we were marriage material or misfortune." He put away the phone, avoiding her gaze. "We were voted marriage material."

Cecily stared at the door as it closed behind him, her heart aching, wondering if she'd misread those signs from the universe.

"Steal!" yelled Adam from his seat in the bleachers. The hot June sun beat down on the baseball game in progress. MacGruder's Marauders versus Kent's

Over-Forty-Niners, two Denver city teams competing in the summer adult league.

Adam wiped the sweat off his brow. "Steal!" he
yelled again at the woman inching off second base
toward third. "Mandy, get the lead out and go for it!"

With a burst of speed, the woman ran, sliding into
third just before the outfielder shot the ball to the
third baseman. She stood, flashed a grin at Adam
before brushing some dirt off her MacGruder's Marauders jersey.

He gave her a thumbs-up while several of her team
mates in the dugout clapped, yelled encouragement.

Adam checked his watch. He'd have to leave soon.
Promised to relieve tonight's bartender who had a
date. Six months ago Adam wouldn't have been
available as tonight would have been his radio talk
show. But after his experiences on *Marriage Material...or Misfortune?*, and losing Cecily, Adam no
longer wanted to play the Stud Man, cajole guys to
join the Stud Club, play soundtracks of blasting
trumpets and squealing girls.

So he'd resigned. Also sacked the weekly wet
T-shirt contests at Home Plate.

Some people called it growing up; Adam called it
learning to respect both sexes.

The regulars at the bar, still wanting a baseball team,
had got themselves organized enough to host a few
fund-raisers. Adam had let the events be held at his bar
on one condition. MacGruder's Marauders had to be
co-ed. And they had to support some city-wide causes.

It had taken some work, but the guys had gradually warmed up to the whole co-ed idea, especially Rodney after falling hard for Shirley Petrovich, a forty-something short-order cook who threw a mean curve ball.

A woman wearing a MacGruder's Marauders baseball cap, and carrying several beers and brats, sat next to him. He scooted a little, making room. He caught the scent of gardenias, the scent achingly familiar.

"Brat?" asked the woman, offering him one.

Her voice was also achingly familiar.

His heart pounding, he turned to look.

Cecily.

Wearing jeans, tennis shoes and an Avalanche T-shirt with the crease marks still in it, she nonchalantly handed him half her snack-bar fare.

"Brat and beer okay?"

He nodded, words escaping him. He stared, unsure whether to kiss her or yell at her or just sit there like a frozen statue, dumbfounded beyond belief.

He finally found his voice. "What in the hell are you doing?"

She looked at the hot dog, looked at him. "Didn't you write in your book that one of the perfect girlfriend's best attributes is to, without asking, do a beers-and-brats run to the snack bar at sports events?"

"Yes, I wrote that. Don't believe it anymore, though."

"Oh." She feigned a pout. "And here I traveled all this way to try and fulfill that fantasy."

He didn't know what was making him more hot and bothered. The blazing sun or Cecily.

"So, you're in town on business?" He took a brat and beer, determined to play this cool despite the fact he was working up a sweat just sitting here.

She made a sound of agreement. "Looking for a place."

Cecily almost felt guilty for toying with him like this. Almost. But she'd wanted to play it low-key in case he carried a grudge after all these months.

Or had fallen for someone new.

Truth was, she was shaking, her pulse roaring in her ears. And to think she'd told *Marriage Material...or Misfortune?* that she wasn't an actress. Oh, if they could see her now as she acted playful, confident.

Adam, is your heart still mine?

"What kind of place?" He took a sip of his beer.

"Somewhere where I can work and live." She took a bite, letting the words sink in.

He slid her a glance. "So, it went well in California."

"I worked hard. Loved being close to my family. Rebuilt Well Suited, thanks to you. Did you get my message?"

He nodded. "It made me proud," he said quietly.

She'd written several times, actually, but he'd never responded. Part of her understood, but another part had hurt. She'd missed him terribly, had thought about him non-stop, until it had reached a point where she'd decided the universe wouldn't put her out of her misery until she confronted the man face to face, discovered if he still cared, still wanted to be together.

"Anyway," she said, trying to sound breezy, "I eventually realized some projects might be better carried out elsewhere."

"Projects," he repeated, those lethal blue eyes studying her.

"Not the jacket business. Another book. This one titled *The Perfect Relationship*. Thought you'd maybe like to co-author it with me."

He nearly choked on his hot dog. "No, thanks. I'm through with setting false standards of perfection."

"Oh, but this book wouldn't be about standards. It'll describe what makes a man and a woman successful *together*."

"And, what's that?" He shot her a perplexed look.

"Compromise." She took a sip of beer.

Adam squinted into the sun, thinking that was what he'd offered her six long months ago and she'd chosen instead to walk out the door. Figuratively speaking. Actually, *he'd* walked out the door that night, and into a life that had felt, at its core, hollow ever since.

But she could have given him some advance warning instead of rushing back into his life with ideas and plans and a *book*.

Then he thought back to that night she'd blurted, "I love you." This wasn't a woman who always paced herself.

"So why now?" he asked.

"Adam," she said, her voice going soft. She shifted to face him, her gaze somber. "When I told you I needed to make Well Suited successful before I could be in a relationship, I was wrong. Instead of being lonely and building my business, I could have been with you, building my business. Best of both worlds."

"Why didn't you?"

"I was afraid to compromise."

He looked deeply into those chocolate-brown eyes that he'd thought he'd never see again and felt a rush of emotion that left him feeling sucker-punched. She'd come all this way to make amends and he'd be a damn fool to not take her up on it.

"The next run for brats and beer is mine," he whispered.

"Yeah?" She smiled, her eyes wet with emotion.

"Yeah." He waggled his fingers, indicating for her to hand him her food and drink. She did, and he set them alongside his on the seat next to him.

"Have you noticed nobody's staring at us as though we're reality TV stars?" he asked. "I think we had our fifteen minutes of fame, and now life in Denver can be relatively normal again."

"You're right, except…" she looked down at the playing field "…they're staring at us."

He looked down. Rodney, Larry, Tom and Vince were lined up outside the dugout, grinning as though they were watching the best show on earth. Vince gave him a virtual high-five.

"Ignore them," he said, turning back to Cecily. "They're just jealous."

He wrapped his arms around her, taking in her scent, the sun glistening off her skin, the way her lips smiled. If any moment in his life was perfect, this was it.

He lowered his mouth, brushing his lips ever so lightly against hers.

"Bradley will make one hell of a wedding planner," he murmured before giving her a kiss to kick off the rest of their lives.

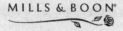

__Modern__
romance™

THE MEDITERRANEAN MILLIONAIRE'S MISTRESS by Maggie Cox

When Lysander Rosakis meets beautiful Ianthe Dane on a Greek holiday, he neglects to tell her that he is a multi-millionaire. Is she in too deep? Not knowing that there is more to be revealed, Ianthe must decide whether to stay, or to turn and walk away...

BY ROYAL DEMAND by Robyn Donald

Gabe Considine, Grand Duke of Illyria, needs revenge. He believes his whirlwind fiancée, Sara Milton, stole a priceless heirloom from him and betrayed him with another man. Now Gabe wants his pride – and his property – back! If he has to seduce Sara into submission, he will...

IN THE VENETIAN'S BED by Susan Stephens

Nell is helpless to resist Luca Barbaro's brand of raw sexuality, but she can never forgive his brutality of years ago. Until they meet again in Venice, not as Luca and Nell, but as two masked strangers in the grip of pure, irresistible attraction...

A FORBIDDEN PASSION by Carla Cassidy

Talbot McCarthy was the only man who fired Elizabeth's passion. He was also her ex-husband's brother, so Elizabeth avoided him. But when Talbot offered his plane to bring her missing son home, and circumstances conspired against them, Elizabeth realised they had to hide their feelings – at all costs...

On sale 7th July 2006

Available at WHSmith, Tesco, ASDA, Borders, Eason, Sainsbury's and most bookshops

www.millsandboon.co.uk

FROM *SUNDAY TIMES* BESTSELLING AUTHOR PENNY JORDAN

They had shattered her past.
Now she would destroy their futures.

Pepper Minesse exuded sexuality and power. She
presented a challenge men wished they could
master. But Pepper had paid dearly for her success.
For ten years, her thirst for revenge had fuelled
her ambition and made her rich.

Now it was time for the four men who had taken
something infinitely precious from her to pay too
– their futures for her shattered past.

On sale 7th July 2006

www.millsandboon.co.uk

M&B